L.S. Hilton is the New York Times bestselling author of the *Maestra* trilogy. Her novels as Lisa Hilton include *The House with Blue Shutters* (shortlisted in the UK for the Commonwealth Fiction Prize), *Wolves in Winter* and *The Stolen Queen*. She was educated at Oxford University and lives in Venice, Italy.

Also by Lisa Hilton

The Real Queen of France:
Athénaïs and Louis XIV

Mistress Peachum's Pleasure:
The Life of Lavinia, Duchess of Bolton

Queens Consort:
England's Medieval Queens

The House with Blue Shutters

The Horror of Love:
Nancy Mitford and Gaston Palewski in Paris and London

Elizabeth: Renaissance Prince

Sex and the City of Ladies

ALL MY LOVERS' WIVES

A Romance

by

L.S. Hilton

Massot Éditions, Paris - London

First published in 2022 by Massot Éditions / Société Éditions du 31 Décembre

17 rue Dupin 75006 PARIS

Copyright © L.S. Hilton, 2022

The moral right of the author has been asserted by her in accordance with the Copyright, Designs and Patents Act, 1988.

All rights reserved.

No part of this publication may be reproduced, stored in a retrieval system, or transmitted in any form or by any means, without the prior permission in writing of the publisher, nor be otherwise circulated in any form of binding or cover other than that in which it is published and without a similar condition including this condition being imposed on the subsequent purchaser.

CONTENTS

PART ONE
1. THE BLACK NOTEBOOK
2. DOMESTIC VIEWS
3. BAKED MEATS
4. LA CLASSE
5. EXPENSES
6. ON THE CIRCUIT
7. BLONDE VENUS
8. BELLE DE JOUR
9. DEPENDING
10. SOFT FURNISHINGS
11. INTERLUDE

PART TWO
12. COMMEDIA AL'ITALIANA
13. ON THE ROAD
14. RETALIATION
15. SINE QUA NON
16. SWEETIELAND
17. ACCEPTABLE IN THE 1980s
18. HAPPY FAMILIES
19. HELLO, GOODBYE
20. OUT OF OBSCURITY
21. TARTS
22. ABSENCE UNDER FIRE
23. THE NOTEBOOK REVISITED

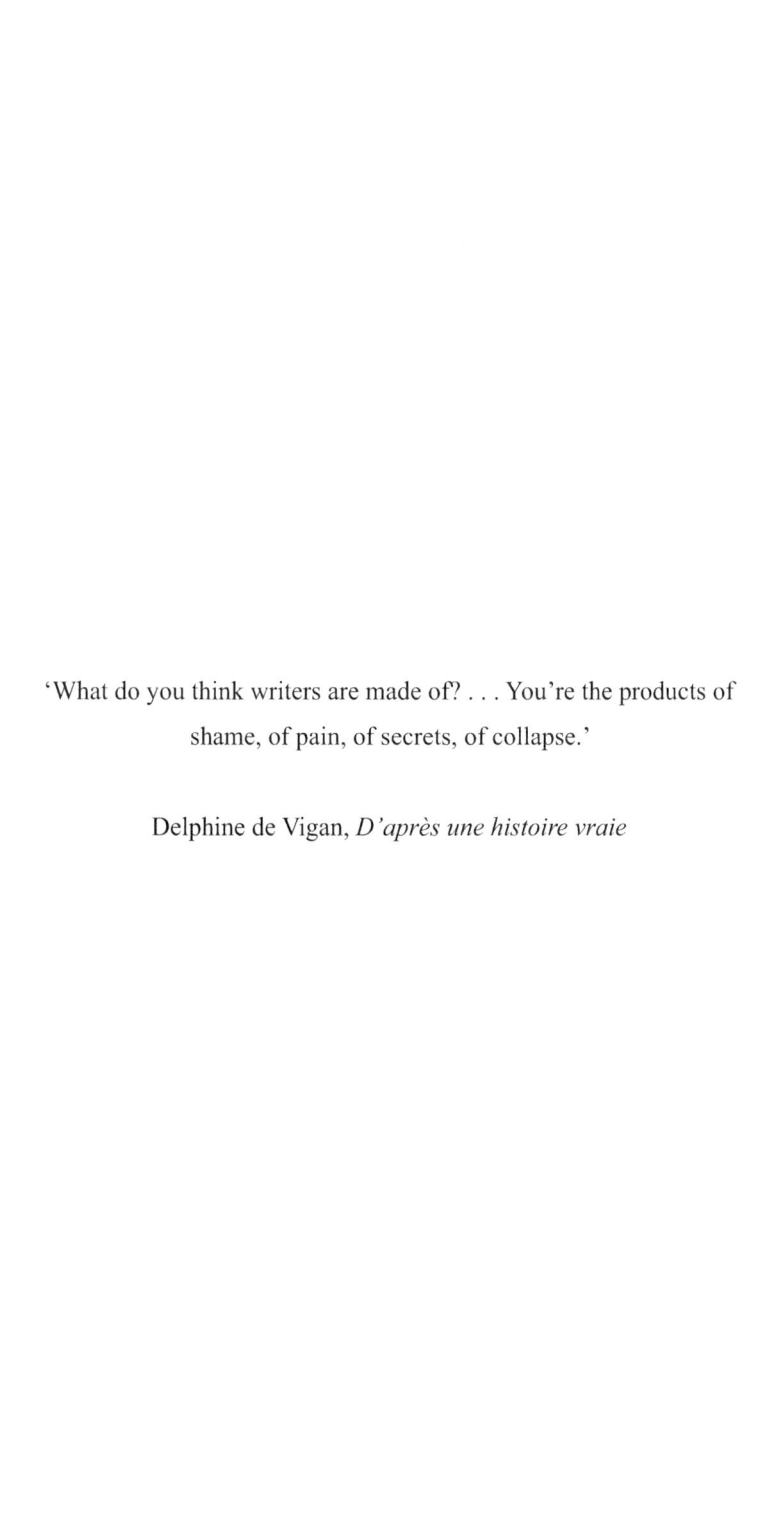

'What do you think writers are made of? . . . You're the products of shame, of pain, of secrets, of collapse.'

Delphine de Vigan, *D'après une histoire vraie*

PART ONE

1. THE BLACK NOTEBOOK

Once, in Venice, I went shopping with B. B was rich, but he found it agonising to spend money. He was choosing a birthday present for his wife. I told him that the handbag he had picked out looked cheap and nasty and wouldn't do. So I took him across the Grand Canal, deep into the alleyways behind Campo San Polo, where I picked out a different bag in glossy conker-brown leather from a tiny workshop. B had to buy it, because he was ashamed. Not of allowing his mistress to choose his wife's present, that is, but of appearing stingy. Some weeks later, I saw B's wife at a book launch in London. She was carrying the bag. It suited her, and that made me glad.

*

I stopped sleeping with married men around the time I stopped writing history books. The two things were connected, in that I had written another kind of book, a novel, which required me to travel a great deal, and that meant I was unable for long periods of time to dedicate myself to married lovers.

Instead, my companion during those months was a single man, who also travelled a great deal. We would meet, in New York or Istanbul or Munich, for a weekend or a few days. It was an arrangement which suited us both, but during those trips, I began to realise that the thing which interested me most about those lost relationships was my former lovers' wives. I knew all about them.

Married men can't help talking about their wives. I knew their secrets, their troubles, while they knew nothing at all about me. I was invisible. I had always liked that, to feel invisible, but because of the novel and the aeroplanes and the journalists who asked me questions and my publishers wanting to me to promote myself online, I couldn't be, at least for a while. I thought about them very often, those women.

Then, about six months after the novel came out, I received a strange email. The address was *anneclarke17@gmail.com* and the sender signed herself — or himself — 'Anne Clarke'. I didn't know anyone with that name.

I was on holiday with a large group of friends in the Marche in Italy. I was disliking myself, because I had rented a big old house near Macerata which was certainly very lovely, but far too expensive, so that every day I woke up there I felt that I was showing off. I also felt stupid, because I had a deadline for another novel and should have been concentrating on that instead of organising dinners and drinking too much wine with my friends, who wanted to stay up late, chatting over cigarettes on the terrace. I have to write early, with a clear head. So I resented them and resented myself for inviting them and then resenting it. Each morning I dragged a small white plastic table into a shady part of the garden and sat there typing while my friends slept guiltlessly, all the time thinking what a stupid and conceited person I had become.

The email said:

To any man who should think of becoming involved with L.S. Hilton: Beware!
Anne Clarke

I am quite used to receiving emails from strangers. Many of them tell me about books they have written or want to write and ask for my help. Others are from students who need information for papers or theses. Still others are straightforwardly complimentary. A number are from angry people who want to tell me that I am a stupid and conceited woman. They repeat certain words: 'slut', 'bitch', 'whore'. I reply to them all. I provide information or suggestions when I am able, I thank the complimentors for their kind words and to the angry I write that it is always encouraging to hear from readers. I sign those, 'Yours faithfully, L.S. Hilton'.

Sometimes I read the book reviews on Amazon, or the comments people have left underneath articles I have written which are republished online. As they are usually very unpleasant, I try not to look too often. I have a friend, an older and very distinguished writer, a wonderful writer, who became deeply distressed when for the first time her work was exposed to such comments. She couldn't understand why people would be so pointlessly malicious. For days, weeks even, she found herself unable to work because she could not stop thinking about the things those people had written about her. I told her that this is just the way things are now — the words 'slut', 'bitch' 'whore' are what we have to expect — and that the only thing is not to look, but that doesn't stop me and I doubt it stops her.

So, Anne Clarke's email was nothing unusual. I even smiled at the exclamation mark. I typed my usual reply and continued to try to write my book, not at all enjoying my grand view and generally feeling very irritated with myself. For some time, I forgot all about it.

*

And then, the next summer, I was once again in Italy. My daughter was staying with her father. The second novel had been published and I had met the man I was there with when he interviewed me about it for an Italian newspaper. He was not married, but he had a girlfriend. They had been together for six years. The man had pretended that he was in Rome for work and the girlfriend had pretended to believe him, but he knew she didn't and she kept telephoning. He spoke to her while he made love to me, while I sucked his cock in front of a six-foot mirror in a yellow Baroque town at the end of Sicily with the hot smell of dust and petrol coming in the window. She telephoned while we were at the beach and while we were at dinner, as we bought peaches at the market or coffee granita on the seafront. I encouraged him to take the calls because that seemed easier than anyone making a scene. I didn't mind. While he spoke to her, except that time I was sucking his cock, I read my book or smoked a cigarette and looked at the twisting spirals of the stone balconies, their intricate curlicues planed smooth by centuries of salt winds.

The apartment where we slept was on the first floor, with a balcony of its own, enclosed, with a columned stone parapet and an arched aperture on to the street. Opposite was yet another balcony in rusted wrought iron, with high narrow wooden doors, swollen and bulging with the heat. They were always shut. After a time, I took to sitting there while the girlfriend was on the phone, with the shutters that gave on to the apartment drawn; that way she couldn't hear me if I moved a glass or clicked my lighter.

Occasionally I caught a word or two as the man lied to his girlfriend. I had spent a great deal of time, I considered, waiting patiently while men lied to their wives. The email I had received from 'Anne Clarke' drifted through my thoughts. Perhaps she might be one of my lovers' wives, those women whose presence I had noticed I missed when I gave up married men? Slowly, an inventory began to unspool in my mind. It wasn't short.

In particular, I began to recall all the details I had heard about Lucy and Emma and Polly, married to H, B and F. My relationships with their husbands had been of some duration, I knew an immense amount about them.

So just then, on that balcony, and I wouldn't be able to write this except that it is true, I received another email from 'Anne Clarke'. The subject line was very clear. It read 'Your affair with my husband'. It continued:

Dear L,

Maybe my email will be of no relevance, or something too irrelevant for you to read. Perhaps you have both decided on where this will go. However, I know you have a daughter and so, as one mother to another, I ask that, no matter how strong your feelings, you now recognise that your decision together about your relationship will profoundly affect my children, our home and our future as a family.

We are here. We were happy.

We now face decisions I hoped we would never have to make. And it will tear us all apart.

The name on the address line was the same as previously. This email was not signed.

The man with whom I was staying tapped on the balcony door and told me he had made reservations for dinner at a place with a terrace on the sea. Like me, he cared a lot about what he ate and apart from the telephoning girlfriend he was generally very thoughtful and considerate. So I went to have a shower and make up my face; afterwards we went out and had some excellent swordfish with fat caperberries and dry Marsala. The man began explaining the plot of a novel he was planning, he wanted to know my opinion. I told him it was a very good idea, but my attention remained with the email. Regardless of who she might be, I realised, I wanted to write about 'Anne Clarke'.

*

I am an adulterous woman. I have never tried to conceal this from my friends. I used to make a joke that the only point of marriage was that it allowed for the possibility of adultery. The only man I never told a lie to thought this was a very funny remark, so much so that he often passed it off as his own. These sharp, brittle jokes were part of a caustic self I had constructed which really had nothing to do with me. Except, given that I said them, they had to be.

So when I began thinking about Anne Clarke, I wondered what might happen if I wrote about my married lovers. If a person writes a memoir about their alcoholism, or the fact that they were sexually abused in childhood, or their bipolar disorder, their anorexia or their mother's suicide, they will be called brave, courageous, a survivor. I knew that this would not be so in my case. I would be called 'bitch,' 'slut,' 'whore'. I would be vilified. Women who sleep with other women's husbands are traitors, the lowest of the low. People would say that I am pathetic, because I have had relationships with married men who did not, in the end, render their own deceit respectable by abandoning their wives and children and leaving with me. They all said they would though. How they begged, how they pleaded, how they swore. But even that, the need to clarify that, sounds defensive and bitter, and that's what people would say.

Anne Clarke had written to me from one side of a divide, and her words made clear my position. Whatever my feelings, implied Anne Clarke, they were not as important as hers. I was not possessed of the same rights as she. She suggested that I might be too cold and unfeeling to see her email as relevant, implying that she, by contrast, was neither. She was in agony. But what did Anne Clarke know about me, or my feelings? Whoever she was, it was not I who had betrayed her relationship with her husband, I could be certain of that. Either he had told her, or she had discovered letters, emails, texts that he had failed to conceal. I had always wanted to remain invisible, but Anne Clarke had discovered me.

I thought of replying to the email. It would be easy to put things straight, to say that Anne was mistaken, that she had written to the wrong person. I even began, 'Dear Anne'. Then I stopped. Anne appeared to think that I was still having sex with her husband. If I suggested to her that I was no longer doing so, it would still imply, obviously, that I had been at some point. Moreover, there were several women who could be Anne. If I mistook her identity, then another relationship could be betrayed. I had an idea of more emails descending on me from these women whom I knew all about. I would be dragged out and punished for all the lies those men had told, thousands and thousands of lies, lies in which I had been entirely and willingly complicit.

When I received the email from Anne while in Sicily, the *Guardian* and the *New York Times*, along with several other broadsheets, were running articles about Jay-Z's new album *4:44*. Everyone knew that on her own latest album *Lemonade*, Jay-Z's wife, Beyonce, had sung about her husband's adultery, with a woman presumed to be 'Becky with the good hair'. One of her songs contained the lyric "He only want me when I'm not there/He better call Becky with the good hair". It was mentioned in all the gossip magazines. In *his* album, Jay-Z apologised to his wife for his behaviour, for not taking her seriously and for putting their marriage at risk. The *Guardian* and the *New York Times* concurred that in addressing his infidelity Jay-Z had not only confronted the painful reality of marital regret but had redirected the art of hip-hop, forcing it to accommodate the emotions of middle age. None of the articles I read speculated on how 'Beckywiththegoodhair' felt about this. I wondered if she read them, and if she minded not receiving any credit for taking hip-hop in a new direction. I wondered how much they'd paid her to keep quiet.

Did Anne Clarke's husband regret his perfidy? Did he blame himself for not taking her seriously and putting their marriage at risk? Probably, if she'd caught him. It was a situation I should have liked to go over with Sebastian, my friend, the man I had never lied to. We used to spend a lot of time dissecting the vicissitudes of our love lives. Sebastian would have given short shrift to pious conventions and sisterly loyalty. He would probably have told me to blackmail the silly cunt and take him to The Ivy on the proceeds. But Sebastian had died.

I didn't want to write to Anne, at least not just yet. I wanted to write about her. My publisher and my agent wanted me to work on another novel, a thriller. I was supposed to be preparing synopses, signing contracts. But I wanted to write about Anne, about all the possible Annes, to see if . . . well, I didn't know quite what the 'if' was.

*

From somewhere, across the sea from Greece perhaps, came the riotous whiff of burning bridges.

*

The next day, I trailed around the shiny marbled streets of that Sicilian town trying to find a notebook. Most of the shops seemed to be permanently closed, and it was extremely hot, but I felt compelled to keep searching, dodging from shadow to shadow.

When I had written history books, I kept my notes and plans in longhand, in a series of hardcover black A4 exercise books. On the front of each, I stuck an Ex Libris sticker, a design with a pale grey silhouette of Françoise-Athenais de Rochechouart de Mortemart, Marquise de Montespan, who had been the titular mistress of Louis

XIV. She was the subject of my first biography. Across the bottom, in cursive script, was my name and Athenais's Latin motto: 'Essere sed videri' *To be and to appear.*

The stickers had been a gift from my ex-husband, he had designed them himself. I still had sheets of them, and each time I extracted a new one, I felt a little stab of pain, brief but acute. I should have stopped using them long ago, but they were reminders of so much — of what he had once believed me to be, of the pain and disappointment we had caused each other. Somehow, I felt it was good for me to think of that, whenever I began a new notebook, so I carried on using the stickers. All the notebooks were piled into a series of leather boxes from John Lewis, so that I could consult them when strangers emailed me with questions, or if I had to prepare a speech or a 'talking head' slot on a television documentary, though since the first novel had been published I had seldom had time for such work. The novels I had written on my laptop.

It had to be a notebook for Anne Clarke. I wanted to feel again the pleasing rhythm of my pen-nib keeping pace with my thoughts, the weight of it in my hand, the satisfaction of the slowly-filling sheets. Eventually, I found a *cartoleria*, and bought a beautiful notebook with a soft black leather cover and heavy ivory pages. That evening, beneath the four ribs of the balcony, I opened it and began to write.

Anne had written 'as one mother to another'. The three women I considered might be Anne, the wives of H, B and F, all had children. None of their names was Anne, nor did any of them have the initial A or C. However, about ten years ago I had contributed an essay on Daphne du Maurier's historical novel *Mary Anne* to a collection called *The Daphne du Maurier Companion*. Mary Anne Clarke was a working- class woman who became the mistress of the Duke of York. In order to maintain the extravagant lifestyle her royal lover casually demanded, Mary Anne began illegally brokering military commissions for cash, a crime for which she was tried and imprisoned. Her scandalous memoirs were a bestseller. A woman who was a mistress, a woman who had written a shocking book- the alias could be a clue, a warning even.

Equally, the fact that I have a child is in the public domain, and my email is probably pretty easy to find. Maybe Anne Clarke was just a random lunatic who liked to email writers accusing them of having affairs with her husband. Perhaps Anne Clarke was a man, or a reader of the *Daily Mail*. Her messages could well be meaningless. Yet if I decided she was real, I could try to give her a shape.

I wanted to do that, in part because the arrangement in that place in Sicily was beginning to give me the pip. The lavatory in the apartment was French-style, that is, separate from the main bathroom. You couldn't pretend you were going in there to do anything else. Many people are quite relaxed about shitting, but I am not. The thought of my farts and the plosive drop of my excrement being overheard, let alone of its smell seeping out under the door, disturbs me. I like to have a shit after breakfast, when I have had coffee and a cigarette. My bowels work excellently; it never takes me long, but I do enjoy privacy. Finding a way of having a comfortable shit is always a concern, and I've often wondered why hotel designers don't take it into account. Since we took our cappuccino and fresh orange juice and brioche at one of the bars in the pale marble square in front of the Duomo, which had a Caravaggio in it, my solution was to excuse myself and swiftly use the lavatory in the bar, but on the first day I was foiled as it was a Turkish shower trench and I couldn't bring myself to open my anus over its stinking, befouled hole. The next time we tried a different bar, with a discreet and satisfactory bathroom, but the third day the man I was staying with said he preferred the coffee at the first bar and I couldn't think of a reason to object. Much as I hate the feeling of swollen heaviness that comes with not shitting I did not feel pleased that taking a crap was set to become the crowning achievement of my day or that I would find myself obliged to pass the time in surreptitious farting. I am quick to spot people who are bad at shitting: the breath of course, and the sheeny purple bags that come beneath the eyes. I rather despise it.

In that part of the island, caves used often to be built onto with bricks to make homes, and, for our last evening, the man had booked a room in one. It had a huge stone bath, big enough for two people to lie side by side full length, sunk into the floor, and a vast white leather couch — the whole placed looked like a James Bond porn set — but it was entirely open plan. You could actually see the lavatory from the bed, and altogether I couldn't wait to leave so I could just go to the loo and then think properly about Anne Clarke.

In the cab on the way home from Gatwick, I replied to her second email:

Dear Ms Clarke,
I am afraid I have no idea who you are, or who your husband might be. Perhaps you have accidentally mistaken me for someone else? I am sorry to be unable to help you.

Yours, L.S. Hilton

Generally, the people who send me offensive emails do not bother to write back once they have received a civil, unruffled response. If Anne did, she was either genuine or more seriously disturbed than the usual correspondent. Her two emails had been sent a year apart. Had she suspected me of an affair with her husband initially and then, twelve months later, learned something which confirmed it?

I unpacked and made dinner, ate it sloppily and pleasurably, and went to bed planning a great gorge of sleep, and looking forward to using my own bathroom in the morning.

2. DOMESTIC VIEWS

My married lovers were, one way or another, writers. In conversation with a friend whose brother-in-law, also a writer, had had an affair, the friend described the woman with whom the brother-in-law had been unfaithful to his wife as 'the kind of person who "does" writers'. She spoke as though fucking writers were something special, even aspirational. I imagine that lawyers fuck lawyers and accountants fuck accountants; it seems quite usual to me to meet men through my job, but perhaps I too am the kind of person who "does" writers.

*

I met H when Sebastian took me to a party at the Ralph Lauren shop on Bond Street. Our friendship had begun years before through *The Sensualist* magazine, a publication which sold itself on a highbrow take on sex. The newsagent W.H. Smith had refused to stock it, creating excellent publicity for the magazine and its writers, one of whom was Sebastian. His column was called 'Gutter Life'. The first time I read it, I thought he was a genius: sharp, funny, witheringly cynical. Amongst other observations on his daily round, Sebastian often wrote about prostitutes, of whose company and services he was very fond, and described how he let his flat in Soho in the afternoons to various working girls in order to pay for drugs and painting materials. He was obliged to become a *flâneur*, wandering the streets for hours while the flat was in use, which necessity provided material for his articles. He had fixed a plaque by the door of his house which read:

THIS IS NOT A BROTHEL. THERE ARE NO PROSTITUTES AT THIS ADDRESS.

I had seen the plaque many times as I walked along Meard Street, without knowing who lived there until I read the 'Gutter Life' column. Later Sebastian told me that one of the prostitutes was a very large lady who specialised in fat fetishism. Sebastian's heroin dealer had done an apprenticeship in carpentry so the next time he delivered a consignment of gear he brought along his toolbox and together they reinforced the bed.

I don't like to think of myself as the sort of person who goes to parties in shops, but there I was, at one. Sebastian had been asked in his persona as London's best-known dandy and had duly turned up in a red sequin suit tailored on Savile Row with his trademark syringe pocket to give the hedge funders a thrill. He had rehearsed his amusing lines with me on the walk from Soho, so we didn't need to talk to one another. I was looking around for someone to speak to when H approached me between the trenches of folded beige cashmere.

I had in fact met H previously, at another party at the Wallace Collection given by my publishers, but I had forgotten, though later I naturally pretended to remember all about it. I think it went like this at the Ralph Lauren shop: H and I chatted for some time — we had many acquaintances in common — and then we spoke about our work. We discussed his books, which I admired, and mine, which he professed to admire. He asked me if I should like to call at his home for a drink one evening and took my number.

*

H lived in a large stucco house in north London. As he let me in, I noticed a silver-framed photograph on the hall table; the smiling couple was him with his wife, Lucy. I recognised her, she was a journalist and I'd seen her around at various launches but she still used her maiden name for her work so I didn't know that they were married. We drank a glass of champagne on the sofa, then H told me he had to attend an event in a bookshop in Piccadilly. I was going that way, so we shared a cab, then walked together a little way down from The Ritz, past Fortnum and Mason, talking all the time. I left him outside the shop and walked up Regent Street, towards home. All the time I was thinking that I felt like someone who has been sitting indoors all afternoon, reading perhaps, and then someone comes in and turns on the light, and only then does one realise that it is twilight outside, that it has begun to get dark without one noticing. My life had become so quietly and insidiously drab I had not seen it, then H had come along and turned on the light. I knew then, quite certainly, that we would have an affair.

Several days later I received a card from H saying how much he had enjoyed our drink, and joking that if he received a knighthood for a book he was working on, he would like me to become 'Lady H'. He also invited me to a dinner where he was giving a speech. I went to the dinner, and afterwards he asked me to have a drink at a club in Mayfair. The place was as quiet as a library, we sat alone in a dim room on the ground floor. I asked for a brandy Alexander. After I had drunk half of it, I knelt down and gave H a blow job.

I swallowed his cum, got up, finished my drink and left without saying a word.

After that, H said he was in love with me.

*

When they can, I find that married men enjoy being unfaithful in their own homes. Perhaps it's the French farce element, amping up the probability of being caught. Or perhaps the urge is something nastier, more infantile, the need to besmirch what is pristine. Quite often, I would take a bus to H's house in the morning and we would have sex in his study. The house had a large back garden with a lilac tree and a hedge of rose bushes, but H's study was on a half landing and overlooked an alleyway and the council wheelie bins. I became quite familiar with that view: in the study, H liked to screw from behind, with me bending over his desk.

Once, after I had left, H's wife returned unexpectedly from a meeting at their children's school. He was reading in the study, there appeared to be nothing amiss, but when she entered the room to speak to him, H noticed that there was a dollop of cum on the parquet floor. It was right next to her shoe. All the time H was speaking to his wife, he had to try not to look at the whitish globule shining there on the floor. Then he thought that she might step in it and slip over. H relayed this story to me because he thought it was hilarious.

I soon made up a nickname for H's wife. I do that a lot with people. At least, it was more of an additional epithet, as I added a word to her Christian name. I called her 'Fragrant' echoing the word used by the judge in the trial of Jeffrey Archer, the bestselling author turned Tory peer. Lord Archer was accused and convicted of perjury after denying in court that he had slept with a certain prostitute, and the judge had questioned whether it was possible for a man to be unfaithful to such a 'fragrant' woman as Lady Archer. "Fragrant" seemed to suit H's wife. She was the kind of woman other women refer to as 'nice'. Each time I had seen her, she had been wearing a skirt. H described Fragrant Lucy as an 'English rose', by which I assume he meant that she was fair skinned. It occurred to me that this label, which was both clichéd and lazy, substituted for H having any thoughts about his wife at all. The name caught on, so much so that H's friends began using it, though never to her face.

Of course, H told me that he and his wife no longer had sex. All married men tell you that. They tell you that they haven't had sex with their wives for a decade and you have to stop yourself answering, 'But you have an eight-year-old.'

Since we frequently fucked in their bedroom, I knew that H's wife didn't think of herself as a woman who didn't have sex, because there was a naked photograph of her on their bedroom wall, and several others strategically positioned in the dressing room and bathroom. They were black and white, very 'tasteful'. They had been shot by a photographer who worked for a vanity studio, where you pay to be made up professionally and photographed with all the right lights and filters. Fragrant Lucy had given the photographs to her husband as a gift on their eldest child's first birthday.

I know what I am supposed to think. I am supposed to think that H's wife was embracing her sexuality and owning her body, that she was celebrating her femininity and that I ought to have been celebrating it right along with her, even when her husband was bucking and sweating on top of me. I didn't think that. I thought they were screamingly awful. Not because H's wife looked bad — she looked very attractive — but because here in her own bedroom, her private space (which her husband was permitting me to invade), she had to keep advertising herself as a sexual being. To whom, exactly, apart from whoever else was occupying her pillow? Did she know her husband's proclivities so well that the photos were meant to act as a challenge, a deterrent? If we screwed with me on top, she looked me straight in the eyes.

*

B was more squeamish about sex in the home. His wife Emma was a banker. They lived in the countryside in Oxfordshire, less than an hour from Marylebone station. Their house was also large, with one wing devoted to guest rooms. B's study was in this part, on the ground floor, and he would fuck me there, also over the desk, but never in the bedroom he shared with his wife. I did learn, however, that the marital chamber featured wallpaper from Osborne and Little, the family firm of George Osborne, the former Chancellor of the Exchequer. B seemed quite proud of this. Once, B invited me to spend the night in the guest wing when Emma was travelling on business. His children were there, but they stayed in their own part of the house. B pretended to go to bed, then slipped through the connecting door to the guest wing and joined me in the bedroom. We did not have intercourse, because B explained, rather abashedly, that Emma was suffering from a yeast infection and that he was fearful of passing it on to me. I didn't ask how this could be the case, since he and his wife never had sex. Later, I thought that B had perhaps caught the infection from another party.

After our night in the guest room, B disappeared to drive his daughter to her riding lesson. His son had left early on his bicycle for a sports practice. While B was gone, I naturally opened the door to the family's part of the house. I explored the drawing room, the dining room and the kitchen. Then I went upstairs and found B's wife's office. It was fascinating to feel like a ghost. As I moved around the space, I experienced a sensation I had not felt for many years, that particular weightlessness associated with childhood dreams, where one floats down staircases and through familiar rooms.

There were photographs of B with his wife, and of them both with the children. There was a bank statement open on top of a filing cabinet. I read it, and saw how much money B's wife had in her current account. Next to the bank statement was a compact from Max Factor in dark burgundy plastic. It held powder foundation. I touched the sponge, wondering why a woman as rich as Emma would use high-street make-up.

Next door to the office was a bathroom. *Vogue* magazine was propped by its spine on the edge of the bath. I could see from the stain in the lavatory that B's wife liked to read magazines on the loo. There was nothing much in the bathroom cabinet except aspirin, so I went softly back down the blue-carpeted stairs and returned to the guest wing to wait for B.

*

The things I was writing in the black notebook I had bought on Sicily were supposed to be helping me to work out who 'Anne Clarke' was. I had been trying to set down events as they happened, that is, in roughly the order in which they occurred. This felt odd to me, because I had only begun to consider that Anne Clarke might be B's wife Emma, or H's wife Fragrant Lucy — I hadn't even got round to F's — when something else came up. It seemed untidy, to write in such an unstructured manner, to record, rather than to arrange, and I thought perhaps I could cheat, make things neater, more agreeable to follow and to read. But that just wasn't how they were.

I had gone to another 'literary' party. There was a time when I went to such things often, because it seemed important to 'network', to get to know people — other writers, journalists, publishers, agents. For a time, there was a certain pleasure in entering a room which had once been full of strangers and which was now populated by people I knew, who kissed me on the cheek and made social remarks. I felt that I belonged somewhere, that because these people recognised and appeared to accept me I must have achieved some measure of success, or at least of validation. After a while I realised that, given the choice, I would much rather stay at home and read in my pyjamas, though I admit that I would have minded if I had not continued to be asked, at least, to the literary parties. That hadn't happened yet.

This party was given to launch a book I had admired, had indeed reviewed very positively for a serious journal. I thought the author was an impressive woman, a formidable scholar, who was always very elegantly dressed. Though I didn't think she would care in the least if I didn't attend her party at a restaurant in Mayfair, I wanted to go. When I arrived my married lovers H and B were already in the room. This did not perturb me.

What did, as I was speaking to two or three people I knew, was the loud voice which said: ' Someone ought to throw a glass of champagne over that woman!'

I looked around. A novelist I vaguely recognised glared at me over the rim of her wine glass whilst the people standing near her tittered uncomfortably. There was no doubt as to whom her remark had been directed. The woman's hair fell around her shoulders in blonde ringlets like a little girl's, which sat discordantly with the troughs of fine wrinkles around her eyes. Her lipstick was a dark burgundy, very sharply pencilled, giving her mouth a grabby look, as though she would nip at her food in little snapping bites, like a terrapin.

As I was wearing a dark-coloured dress, it wouldn't matter if someone did throw a glass of champagne over it. I felt suddenly excited, sparky with adrenaline: what would I do if the woman made good her threat? I thought that I would quietly hand my wine glass to the person standing next to me, and then I would punch the woman in the face. Not a girl's punch, a cack-handed halfslap, but a proper punch, thumb curled over the index finger, moving the weight from the hip, not the bicep. She would stagger, probably fall, and then I would stoop over her, as the gossip writers tapped at their phones, and grab her hair to pull her head back, and put my fist under her jaw, positioned ready for an uppercut. And then I would ask her, in a very calm way, if she wanted any more. And when she shook her head, wide-eyed, I would let her go and glide beautifully away. This fantasy, which gave me immense pleasure, was no more than a flash.

Of course, had the woman really thrown the glass, I should have done no such thing. The babble of the party, momentarily silenced by her comment, soon resumed, and nothing more was said. I didn't know the woman's name, but I was certain it was not Anne Clarke.

In my sudden fantasy, I had reacted the way the character in my novels would have done. She was an enraged young woman, bold, fearless, adept at violence, unfazed even by murder. I did share something with her; in reality I am very physically strong, compared with many women, and I move quickly, but I would have been entirely unable to wrench those blonde curls away from that neat little gash of burgundy lipstick. I should have been dismayed, at a loss, perhaps burst into tears.

Shortly afterwards, I left the party and joined some friends for dinner. After we had ordered, I went to the loo and texted B, asking him if he would like to meet. He replied immediately. I think that B had loved me more than the other two men who might have been married to Anne Clarke, and I cared for him least of the three, which made him the right person to call when I couldn't face going home alone. When he arrived in a taxi outside the restaurant, we both behaved as though hardly any time had passed since we last met.

After we had gone through the motions of sex in my bed, I brought B a glass of whisky. I had poured myself a much larger one, downstairs, and drunk it quickly so the levels in the glasses appeared the same. We discussed the woman at the party, how unnerving I had found her remark. B was immediately on guard. Could the glass-throwing novelist know about our past affair? We two had been there, in the same room, so what had she been insinuating? She did not know B's wife, Emma, but perhaps she enjoyed making scenes in public, spreading scandalous stories. Bookish London is a gossipy, provincial village, so if there were rumours that I slept with married men, she might think I deserved to be taken down a peg or two.

I could see B's thoughts as clearly as the shadows thrown on my ceiling by the candle next to my bed. Might the woman contact Emma? I was certainly not the first woman with whom B had had an affair, and indeed I knew that he had another girlfriend now. Yet B clearly felt that the woman's words were directed at him. I found myself reassuring B. There could be many reasons why she had spoken that way, I said soothingly, none of them to do with him. Emma was ignorant of my existence and would remain so. I did not mention Anne Clarke.

B showered carefully and dressed and, when the front door banged, I lay back on my pillows and finished his whisky.

Despite what I had said to B, I was in no doubt that what I had heard that evening *was* in some way connected with the accusatory messages from Anne Clarke. I had written this much about Lucy and Emma in the black notebook when she replied to my email.

I read her words feeling oddly exhilarated:

Dear L,

I didn't want you not to realise that you, personally, have been responsible for a huge amount of suffering on my part, and perhaps that of my children. Everyone should be accountable for their actions. Please go to sleep remembering that and I hope that in your future dealings you bear my words in mind.

This time her email was signed.

Yours, Anne Clarke

3. BAKED MEATS

When I was eight years old, my parents took my sister and me camping in the north of Spain. It took us two days to drive down England, across France and over the Pyrenees, sitting up high on folded sleeping bags, every corner of the car packed with camping equipment. My mother told me recently — and not unkindly — that I frequently embarrassed her at that age by refusing to speak to people. All I wanted to do was read. Apparently during that holiday I told my mother that I saw no point in making conversation with adults, or for that matter the other children on the campsite with whom my mother tried to encourage me to play. When we went to the beach, I would take my book and a towel and walk along the bay. I never seemed to get thirsty in those days. At the end of the main beach was a series of coves, each giving on to another, smaller, beach, until the sequence ended with a pebbled area no larger than a double bed. The rocks which divided the coves were quite high, but I was an excellent and fearless climber, and I liked it that the sharp stones and steep drops meant that neither my younger sister nor any of the other children were likely to follow me. The last rock formation, above the bed-sized beach, had a flat place on the top where I would lay out my towel and read. I liked being there, high up, unseen; invisible. I loved, and still love, climbing trees, hiding at the very top, concealed by the branches.

*

One day, I looked down into the little cove and saw a man lying naked on the shingle. He seemed to be asleep, but he must have sensed my movements because he opened his eyes and looked at me. Quite slowly, he began to touch his penis, until it stood up away from his body. He had very short hair, it was difficult for me to tell his age. I knew what a penis was, but I had never seen one sticking up. It looked ugly and raw, purplish and glistening, exactly like the sea slugs my sister and I dived for. They seemed to spend their lives rolling about pointlessly on the sandy sea bed, but if you could bring yourself to squeeze their warty middles you could use them like a water pistol. The man rubbed and pulled at the penis, looking up at me all the time. After a few moments, I climbed down the rock and returned to my parents on the big beach. I did not tell anyone what I had seen, but not because I was frightened or ashamed. I had not been either frightened or ashamed. It was not until I wrote this down in the black notebook that I found the word for what the man and I had shared: complicity.

'Deceitful' can be a grand word, a clever and sinuous word. 'Furtive' is small and ugly, a rat of an adjective. Neither are nice. When I read Anne Clarke's third email I thought of both those words. Whoever's husband Anne Clarke was referring to, I had been both deceitful and furtive in my relations with him.

Complicity though, complicity puts you somewhere else. I did not feel sexually excited by the sight of the man's penis on the beach, but I think that what I sensed, already at the age of eight, though I couldn't have articulated it then, was power. By my silence I had done more than condone his behaviour, I had conspired in it. As I gazed down at him, tugging and panting, I had power, I felt strong. Complicit in his transgression, I was untouchable. We both knew it, and we each knew that the other knew.

*

I had transcribed the emails from Anne Clarke into the black notebook. She had written that she was suffering, and that in some obscure way, it was in my power to be instrumental in her future, and that of her children. This latter was entirely untrue, so far as I could see. People cheated on one another all the time, it might be experienced as an enormity by the person deceived, but it was a mundane activity none the less.

Anne Clarke had not given an opinion about whether her husband was accountable for *his* actions. She insisted that I was "personally" responsible, as though he had been passive, as though my affair with him was something imposed on him, yet whatever we had done we had done it together. Infidelity is not necessarily an aberration prompted by loneliness or unhappiness or neglect. People cheat because they are greedy, because they want more than their share, not only of sex but of secrets. The staging and choreography of sexual betrayal, the clandestine meetings, the strange beds, the whole ritual of it all can be intoxicating, yet if a woman admits to finding it so, she is judged as abhorrent.

The American novelist Jay McInerney wrote that men need four things: food, shelter, pussy and strange pussy. How would that sound if you flipped it? Might women need cock and also strange cock? 'A bit of strange' used to be slang for a mistress: 'a bit on the side', 'a bit of the other'. It may well have been torture for Anne Clarke to imagine her husband with another woman, but I couldn't see that I was personally rather than generally responsible for her suffering. I had been 'a bit of strange', part of a group of women selected by whichever spouse Anne's proved to be, since what H, B and F had in common, apart from being writers, was that they were all serially unfaithful to their wives.

*

I used to go to tea with Sebastian, usually on a Tuesday. I would buy cakes from Maison Bertaux in Greek Street and we would eat them overlooking the street from the window seat of his flat. Sebastian was fond of a vanilla slice, not a delicate French *millefeuille* but the English version with stiff slabs of primrose-yellow custard and thick white icing on the top. I usually went for a coffee éclair. Sebastian had a long list of things which he did not consider to be 'stylish pursuits' and any form of cookery was one of them, so there was never any food in his kitchen, but he was prepared to go so far as a cup of tea. Sometimes, when I rang the bell, he wouldn't come down, and the black shutters that gave on to the street would be closed. That meant he was using heroin, and I would know better than to disturb him. But mostly in those years when he was clean we talked a great deal, about ourselves and our feelings, like teenagers.

I tried to explain to Sebastian that I thought sometimes that I was set wrong, that I didn't seem to have have the feelings or reactions that most women had. Things that I was supposed to mind or get angry about, I just — didn't. I never felt very real to myself. Sebastian said there was nothing whatsoever 'real' about him, so what was I going on about? — yet I didn't fully believe him. On those Tuesdays, he wouldn't be dollied up in his dandy costume, the crazy suits and outsized top hat; instead he would wear a ragged shirt, its foxed cuffs falling over his thin hands, and an old paint-stained jersey.

After tea we often read aloud to one another, sitting on the floor. Sebastian was an autodidact, tremendously well read but unsystematic; there were gaps in his canon which it rejoiced me to fill. I told him about Professor Nuttall, who had taught me the poetry of John Wilmot, the Earl of Rochester, at university. Wilmot's work has a reputation for being filthy, which much of it is, but the deep intellect behind his craftsmanship, its bleak beauty, is superlative. Sebastian particularly liked the poem 'To the Postboy', with its coruscating final line, 'The readiest way [to hell] my Lord's, by Rochester.'

Sebastian and I were very alike, but I had pegged ballast balloons to my life, so that the wrongness wouldn't get to me the way it did to him. We considered at length the reasons for our mutual sense of being set wrong, and although we never came to any conclusions, it remained a fascinating topic, all the more so, we agreed, for being so immature and self-indulgent. Equally, we shared a contempt for reasons, for giving causes for things — *I'm like this because such and such happened to me*, the whole inescapable Freudian crassness.

I had tried to explore this idea further in the novel I had written, but my editors didn't care for it. They wanted to know why the character was the way she was and said I couldn't be nebulous. If readers didn't have reasons, they couldn't empathise, they said. I answered that men didn't have to give reasons, whereas women are expected to justify and explain their choices and behaviours. Women cannot own their own natures in the way that men are permitted to do. If they behaved badly, whether in history or fiction, there always had to be a motive, a trauma which rationalised it. I said this all the time, in articles, in interviews, in questionnaires that were sent from Spain or Bulgaria. Men could just be. Readers seemed able to empathise with that just fine.

Sebastian said: 'Yes, darling, but look at me. I just sit here, making things and breaking things.'

There were many reasons why I loved Sebastian and not just because underneath the posturing he was immensely generous and kind. He made me feel peaceful as no one else ever had because he was so mercilessly honest, possessed of a lucid quality that went beyond knowing how ridiculous he often seemed. I loved him, but I was scared of his life. It could so easily have been mine, and even then, I doubted I could have carried it off so well. So Anne Clarke wanted me to go to sleep knowing how I had wounded her, and I had wounded her because I was set wrong. That man's penis on the beach probably had something to do with it, but not everything to do with it.

*

I decided I had to be more systematic in my approach to writing about Anne Clarke and my lovers' wives. Turning to a fresh page in the black notebook, I wrote 'Polly' at the top, underlining the name neatly. Next to that, I wrote the dates of my affair with F,

Polly's husband, an exercise which required me to go back to the date-diaries I keep in the top drawer of the bureau next to the front door of my flat. I am a neat person, in that respect at least. The diaries are all the same, repurchased annually from the Smythson concession in Selfridges, each with an identical monogrammed turquoise-blue cover. I repeated the process with Emma and Lucy. The dates overlapped, making it more difficult to guess who Anne Clarke might be.

*

I met F at Sebastian's funeral. At least, I didn't really meet him to speak to, but he was there and he told me afterwards that that was when he had seen me for the first time, though he had known of me much earlier, through reading one of my history books. At the service, I was to give a reading from Sebastian's book of memoirs, *Dandy in the Underworld*. I didn't do it well. Before me, the famous actor Stephen Fry had given a speech. His voice was sonorous and polished, entirely controlled. He was simultaneously impressive and moving. I was not. I was poleaxed by disbelief that Sebastian was in the coffin which had been carried up the aisle of the church in St James's, and I was horribly frightened. My voice wavered and squawked as I read. Halfway through I began to sob. I was shaking and sweating; moreover, I was wearing a fitted black dress with a very tight corset. I was glad of the corset, in that it held me straight when I thought that I might pitch forward, wailing, on those elongated paving stones which had seen so many tears that they are washed in indifference, but, equally, it constricted my diaphragm to the extent that my voice which is quiet at the best of times, was, I think, inaudible, aside from the staccato squeaks.

When I saw F properly, Sebastian was present once again. His heirs had organised a retrospective exhibition of his pictures at a gallery in Greek Street. The proceeds were to go to charity, to the rehabilitation centre where he had tried to kick his heroin habit. Given that he'd died of an overdose, I couldn't see that there was much to celebrate in their work.

I didn't stay long, indeed I was leaving, when a great friend of Sebastian's stopped me and introduced me to F. We were outside, on the pavement, not far from where I had seen Sebastian for the last time. He had been wearing his white suit that evening. I would never forget. We said the usual half-awkward, overly sincere things people say at such gatherings. I had read one of F's books at that point, but I can't remember if I mentioned it. I went away and got drunk in a bar in Lexington Street.

*

After Sebastian died, I was drunk for a year.

*

It took me some time to discover the existence of F's wife, Polly. Sebastian's death had put a temporary stop to my affair with H, and B was not yet in the picture.

The day Sebastian's body was found, I was with H in an hotel in Park Lane. It was not the hotel where we customarily arranged to spend the afternoon in bed. That was in St James's, on a corner near the London Library a few steps from the church where Sebastian's funeral took place. The hotel was popular with adulterous couples because it had two entrances on different streets, ideal for discreet meetings. It was a particular favourite with writers, because they could tell their wives they were working in the stacks at the Library. Membership is required to enter the reading rooms, and there is a strict rule that mobile phones must be switched off. So it's one of the few places in London where you can disappear for a while. But, that day, H had booked a room at the Park Lane Hilton.

We made love and chatted and made love again, and then H brushed my hair. He liked to do that at the end of our encounters. Then he dressed and left. There is a particular pain associated with that sensation, when your lover leaves you alone on the stained sheets and goes back to his everyday life. It is squalid and clichéd and altogether dreadful. Before I had a shower, I checked my phone. It was full of missed calls and messages. Sebastian had been found dead of the overdose, naked and alone in his flat. Friends were gathering in a café across the street, waiting for news, waiting for the body to be brought out. I called H immediately to tell him what had happened. I hoped that he might come back for a while, perhaps accompany me the short distance to where Sebastian's body was being lifted on to a stretcher. I had never asked anything like that of him before. I had made no kind of emotional demand. H said how sorry he was, but he was rushing off to a meeting about a literary festival. Then he had to meet Fragrant Lucy for dinner. For a long while I sat naked at the end of the hotel bed, staring at the sky over Hyde Park, with my phone in my hand as it buzzed and vibrated.

The disappointment I felt in H was more present, more real, than the fact that Sebastian was a corpse. It was familiar, manageable.

*

I hadn't really registered F's name when we were introduced because of having been drunk and having gone on being drunk. I had told my friends that I had broken up with H. I let them think that it was because I had come to my senses and realised there was no point in having affairs with married men, but it wasn't quite like that. I was too ashamed to tell them of the way he had behaved over Sebastian. In the way that happily married friends do, they tried to set me up with people, once I'd knocked off the sauce. The friend who arranged for me to have dinner with F didn't realise that he was married. She had enjoyed several of his books and had recommended them to me, observing that the 'author bio' on the back cover said simply that F lived in London, no mention of a wife. However, my friend had learned that F had children and she therefore assumed he had been widowed. Not because he had told her so, but because he conspicuously wore two wedding rings and spoke frequently of his two children, but never of their mother. My friend retained what she believed was a tactful, sensitive silence.

F was late to the dinner. When he arrived, my first thought was, 'Oh, it's you.' My second thought was that he was balding, which I hadn't seen the first time, in the street in Soho, as he had been wearing a cap. The fourth in the party, my friend's boyfriend (I hate the word 'partner'), is a chef, so for much of the evening we talked about food.

*

B's wife, Emma, turned out to be a functional anorexic in the way that some people are functional alcoholics, that is, she wasn't what a 'healthy' person would deem functional at all. On the other hand, she got up in the mornings. It made perfect sense to me.

Emma weighed herself obsessively, and if the bathroom scales crept up by so much as half a pound, it could provoke a crisis. Frequently, she would refuse to attend parties or other social commitments because she felt too 'fat'. Her job was in part a source of agony, as banking involved so many lunches and dinners. Emma's strategy was to secrete low-calorie diet bars in her handbag, which she would consume locked into a lavatory cubicle before a business event involving food. This would prevent her being tempted to guzzle the scallops or the rack of lamb, which she could just push around her plate as though partly eaten. The fashion for allergies and intolerances proved a gift to her. Emma could say that she was intolerant of practically everything except salad without overstepping the bounds of social acceptability. No one ever appears to be allergic to salad. Emma pretended to enjoy drinking because it's a big part of the banking culture and also because her husband B professed to be knowledgeable about wine. Her strategy there was to 'share' B's drinks at parties, which gave her an excuse to remain near him at all times, taking invisible sips from his glass. This didn't appear especially irritating to B.

H's wife, Fragrant Lucy, also had 'issues' with food. Whilst hers were not so pronounced as Emma's, she kept a rigorous watch on her figure and was proud that she remained the same weight as on her wedding day. H told me this several times. Fragrant Lucy did not really like to eat at family meals — H described her as a 'nibbler'. I thought of them, Emma and Lucy, secretly gobbling. Emma confidently controlled billion-pound accounts and thousands of employees, Lucy was so accomplished, so polished. I knew all the myriad reasons why controlling food could be a means of managing distress, but I was curious as to why these particular women needed to. I wondered why they wanted to make themselves so small. I wondered why their husbands appeared tacitly to approve of this, or at least to accept without question that not eating was just something women do.

*

At that dinner it felt as though both F and I were trying to be brilliant, to impress one another. The longer the evening went on, the more it seemed as though it was just the two of us, that my friend and her boyfriend were witnesses to a private performance. We were flirting, but it felt, to me, refined. Intellectual flirting. When I eventually left the restaurant, I knew that F was interested in me. There was a sparkle in the cab lights as they caught the puddles in Mount Street, sliding oiled jewels of refracted possibility.

    F was not strictly a handsome man, but he was the kind who can 'talk away his face'. I thought, deliciously, that we were going to fall in love. I had sensed the thought before it crystallised, because when you fall in love, you feel the pavements dancing.

    My friend agreed that the evening had gone very well. She told me on the phone that F was clearly attracted to me. We would be 'perfect', together, she said. Her encouragement made me hopeful.

F wrote me a postcard. I still had it; I was looking at it as I wrote in the black notebook. It was a print from the Hogarth series *The Rake's Progress*, pictures I had written about in my second history book. It was signed 'Your secret friend'. The companion series to *The Rake* is *The Harlot's Progress*. Neither story ends well.

4. *LA CLASSE*

Whilst adultery was an accepted fact in the lives of H, B and F, each of them approached it differently. When I thought about it, I decided that this came down to their respective places in the class system.

H and his friends had all been educated at famous public schools. They were entirely open with one another, and indeed with me, about their infidelities. They took a collegiate approach to adultery, sharing flats for assignations and frequently the women they had them with. Lovers were divided into mistresses, or as H liked to speak of it, 'love affairs', and 'girls'. 'Girls' were usually very pretty, very young, and had the sense to act as though they were quite stupid. They floated around on the social scene, being passed from one man to another. Mistresses were longer standing relationships, such as the one I shared with H. Girls and mistresses were treated very politely, and it was taken as a given that a man in H's circle would be financially magnanimous, though it seemed that the girls did rather better out of that than the mistresses, in terms of time engaged.

Then there were tarts. H, and all his friends, used tarts very openly and naturally. They departed for the brothels of Knightsbridge or Pimlico after all-male dinners, gleefully plotting which woman they would select, passing on tips and recommendations the way women do about, say, beauty therapists. H's wife, Lucy, clearly knew that he frequented prostitutes. She had had a hysterectomy due to complications after the birth of her last child, H told me, but none the less insisted that they use condoms whenever they had sex. Although obviously, they never had sex. I was curious about this paradox. Not the never having sex, which was just the familiar lie, but how one could engage in such an intimate act and use a condom, without ever admitting why. Basically, every time they fucked, Lucy was telling H she knew about the tarts and H was admitting it, but neither of them ever said so.

H always said "Thank you, darling" to me after we had finished having sex. Upper-class men always say "thank you" because they can never quite rid themselves of the idea that sex is something nasty men do to women who aren't professionals. I knew he said it to Lucy too, after they hadn't had sex.

B had not been educated at a famous public school and nor (unlike his wife) had he been to Oxbridge. He mentioned this frequently, each time professing that he was glad because he knew more about the 'real world'. Obviously, he minded very badly, or else he wouldn't have carried on mentioning it. H and his friends were unselfconsciously 'posh', whilst B's background, though monied, was more middle class. I think this was why he also told me frequently that he had never had to pay for sex, as though paying for it wasn't exactly the reason you pay for it.

B had always had girlfriends. He told me that he had slept with more than a hundred women, which he obviously expected me to find impressive and rather shocking. I was duly impressed and shocked. B recounted many of his sexual adventures to me — the Dutch book publicist, the Italian publishing assistant, the American fixer. I noted that where the encounters had taken place abroad, when B was travelling on book promotions, their subjects were always younger and less powerful than B. In England, B had had several long-standing affairs, including one with the editor of a magazine I had written for. He had given her a necklace with a diamond pendant for her birthday, and once, at a dinner given by the magazine in a museum, I recognised it from his description, shining between her collarbones. I imagined her in bed with B, his hands fastening the necklace on, and thought of all the strange ways in which adultery connects people, though they seldom know about it.

B was convinced that Emma knew nothing about his affairs. He was meticulous in the construction of alibis and never failed to phone Emma each evening when he was away on a trip with me. This caused some awkwardness when the Facetime app came into use. B didn't tell me he was Facetiming Emma and I walked across the room naked while he was doing it. He signaled to me frantically and I dived under the sofa of the Amsterdam hotel room. I had to stay there the whole time he was telling Emma about the weather and what the fictitious dinner he had attended the previous evening had been like. It was cold under the sofa, but the carpet was very clean.

F's approach was different again. Unlike H and B, for whom extra-marital relationships were a contained, separate part of life, F was incontinently, greedily promiscuous. He'd have fucked a bucket with a hole in it if it had been wearing a skirt. His persona was something he had constructed, won — I think it is fair to say — against the odds of a childhood in a bookless home on a council estate, but unlike B, he wasn't socially anxious or awkward. He acted the part of an unrepentant sensualist very successfully in his writing, but when I tried to categorise his private approach to sex, I found myself thinking of the Alan Sillitoe novel *Saturday Night and Sunday Morning*. No one reads Sillitoe much any more, but what I remembered of the book was a sense that its working-class protagonist was both drawn to and infuriated by sex. He experienced it as a compulsion and a trap, the embodiment of everything he felt he had a right to and yet which he was prevented from enjoying freely by his social circumstances. F was angry.

*

My fifth book was a dual biography of the English writer Nancy Mitford and her lover of twenty-nine years, the French politician and diplomat Gaston Palewski. The title was *The Horror of Love*. The book argued that Nancy Mitford's popularity diminishes her in something of the same manner as does Jane Austen's. Bonnets and bosoms in Jane's case, diamonds and darlings in Nancy's. Innumerable film and television representations of both women's work have tended to emphasise what Austen herself termed the 'light, bright and sparkling'. Yet there is a toughness, a darkness in their novels, handled so dexterously that the lightness of their touch almost disguises their very real capacity to convey pain, loss and hopelessness. Nancy Mitford's first two post-war bestsellers deal respectively with a serial adulteress who dies in childbirth and a sexually molested child who marries her abuser and destroys her family in the process. They might be read as part of the attenuated tradition of the English Gothic novel whose inception Jane Austen had satirised in *Northanger Abbey*.

Nancy Mitford settled permanently in France after the war, first in a flat in the seventh arrondissement, which was by all accounts enchanting, and later in Versailles. The novels she wrote in the 1950s, *The Blessing* and *Don't Tell Alfred*, are fairytales of Gallic didacticism whose pragmatism contrasts with the wilder, romantically violent loves which lurk beneath the glittering surfaces of *The Pursuit of Love* and *Love in a Cold Climate*. As her relationship with Gaston Palewski continued, Nancy's perspective on love became progressively more 'French' or perhaps rather more eighteenth century. The keystones of her romantic philosophy became civilisation and adulthood, revealing the potential of an intimacy based upon ideas which many contemporary women would find frankly appalling. Fidelity is not the point of marriage, though it may well be the end; adultery, if properly managed, may be a highly refined activity (despite the tiresomeness of always having to go to bed in the afternoon), and the one essential for happiness is not self-exposure or mutual dependency but great good manners.

As part of the unsentimental education of *The Blessing*, the discovery of a husband's infidelity is presented as an engaging, even joyful opportunity:

"It is quite different for a Frenchwoman, she has ways and means of defending herself. First of all, she is on her own ground, and then she has all the interest, the satisfaction, of making life impossible for her rival. Instead of sad repining her thoughts are concentrated on plot and counterplot, the laying of traps and the springing of mines.

Paris divides into two camps, she has to consider most carefully what forces she can put in the field, she must sum up the enemy strength and prepare her stratagem.

Whom can she enlist on her side? There is all society to be won over, the hostesses, the old men who go to tea parties, and the families of those concerned. Then there is the elegance, the manicurists, the vendeuses, *the* modistes, *the* bottiers *and the* lingeres. *A foothold among the tradesmen who serve her rival's kitchen may prove very useful; we must not, of course, forget the fortune tellers, while a concierge may play a cardinal role.*

The day is not long enough for all the contrivances to be put on foot, for the consultations with her women friends, the telephoning, the messages, the sifting and deep consideration of all news and all fresh evidence."

It sounds a delightful activity. Who wouldn't want to be speeding around Paris in nine metres of Dior skirts conducting a duel to the death of glamour and wit? The shimmer and bounce of the prose almost deflects other readings. The language used is military: 'mines', 'camps' 'forces', enemy','enlist' — the vocabulary of a masculine, martial sphere arrogated to the feminine realm. Perhaps one might suggest that this is indicative of the trivialisation of women's existence in the culture of the 1950s, that after the emancipation imposed by the exigencies of wartime they were being relegated to their proper, domestic space, their battles diminished to the emotional and decorative. Or perhaps Nancy is touching on the human need to reassert agency in the face of deceit. Infidelity renders the deceived disoriented and powerless, obliges them to acknowledge an entirely different reality from that which they believed themselves to inhabit.

An obsessive desire to *know*, to investigate and assess all aspects of the individual who has reconfigured our world, is ancient and elemental, even if the sense of renewed autonomy it provides is ultimately illusory. The Internet makes it that much easier.

*

I had caught up with my notes on these three of my lovers' wives on the day I took my daughter to the National Gallery. We often went there on Sundays: afterwards we'd walk down to Fortnum and Mason. First, we would examine the window displays thoroughly, then go inside to choose one perfect, luxurious truffle apiece from the chocolate section. A single silver almond *dragee* was bought for my daughter's doll, Emmeline, who came everywhere with us. We would suck the chocolates, slowly, as we walked through St James's, looking into the windows of the galleries. I would ask my daughter what she noticed about the pictures on display, when they were made or where they might have come from. There is an old-fashioned phrase for being able to identify paintings in this way — 'knowledge of hands'. I felt proud when my daughter got the answers right. Then we would cross into Green Park and walk over to St James's Park. When she was little, I would push her on the swings, and then we would visit the pelicans. My daughter knew that these absurd, majestic birds had first been given royal sponsorship when the City of London had presented one as a gift to Anne of Bohemia, the first bride of the doomed Plantagenet king Richard II. The pelican symbolised the queen's devotion to her people, as in times of scarcity the mother bird will open her own breast with her beak to feed her young with her blood. I enjoyed walking and chatting with my daughter like this, partly because of the pleasure it gave us both (at least, I hoped it gave her pleasure) and partly because it made me feel as though I was being a good mother, stimulating and paying attention to my child.

That particular day, we had spent a long time looking at the Uccello of St George and the dragon. I explained to my daughter that saints in old pictures are usually identified by a symbol — St Jerome with the lion, or St Sebastian with the arrows. George is an easy one, because of the dragon. Then we followed our usual routine. My daughter chose a pink champagne truffle in Fortnum's. I warned her that she wouldn't like the alcoholic taste, but the colour was so pretty, a sherbet rose, that she couldn't resist. On the way to the park, we swapped our half-sucked chocolates, my salted caramel for her champagne strawberry. There are moments when you feel such an access of love for your child — they hand you a melted chocolate, dripping with brown saliva, and though it would be revolting from anyone else, you pop it gladly in your mouth because you know that one day the time will come when they won't want to do that anymore.

In the park, it began to rain hard, so we took a black cab home as a treat. When I opened the front door of my flat, there was a postcard lying on the doormat. Odd. It was Sunday, no post. The postcard was from the shop at the National Gallery, the illustration was the Uccello St George.

My daughter was struggling to take off her wet shoes. I snapped at her, told her to hurry and go to her room to get on with her homework. I carried the postcard into the kitchen, holding it gingerly by its edges. I checked my phone, 4 p.m., too early for a drink. I put the kettle on and made a cup of tea. Then I lit a cigarette and turned the postcard over.

The message was printed in Biro. It said:

I hope you had a lovely time with your daughter, L. AC.

*

An actress friend once told me that one of the more difficult physical things to play realistically is vomiting. She described holding a mouthful of cold Heinz vegetable soup in her mouth between takes for a television comedy, ready to spew it out at the correct moment. I thought of that as I went upstairs to the bathroom, closed and locked the door, flipped up the loo seat, knelt and flushed, so that my daughter would not hear me retching. The bile surged out, smooth beige, tea and chocolate truffle. When I stood up, I was breathless and dizzy and very cold. I brushed my teeth and squirted Cillit Bang from the cupboard under the sink into the bowl, wiping round carefully to remove splashes of sick from the underside of the seat. I washed my hands. All the while I was performing these activities, I was aware that they were procrastinations, that if I could concentrate sufficiently on the Cillit Bang, the soap, the toothpaste, I would not have to think about the fact that Anne Clarke knew where I lived.

*

I had thought I was invisible, but Anne Clarke knew my address. She had not followed me back home from the National Gallery, trailing my cab through the greasy London rain, since the postcard had been there when I returned. Therefore, Anne Clarke must either have been waiting in the street for me to leave my flat with my daughter, followed us to the gallery, bought and written the card and delivered it before I got back, or had, by coincidence, seen us in the gallery, bought and written the card and delivered it before I got back. Either way, Anne Clarke had prior knowledge.

Or perhaps Anne Clarke had seen us at the National Gallery some other Sunday, followed us home and stored the information for another visit. Perhaps Anne Clarke had followed me back from somewhere else entirely, the gym or the library or the Tube station. In short, Anne Clarke's knowledge of my address opened up the possibility that I had been spied upon for some time. Someone had been observing me, dodging in and out of doorways, perhaps wearing a disguise.

The idea of a disguise brought me up short. I couldn't imagine Emma or Polly or Lucy lurking outside in a wig or a false pair of glasses. It was farcical. So 'Anne Clarke' must be a nutter of some kind, not a stalker lurking online but a real person, abroad in the streets, watching.

*

Some years previously, my publisher had received a parcel addressed to me. As distinct from the anonymous individuals who abuse me online, people who bother to send packages — who have invested the time in discovering who publishes my books, where the office is, who go to the post office, queue up and pay to send something — tend to be amiable. I had received books and magazine articles this way, or the occasional handwritten fan letter, even flowers or bottles of wine.

This parcel contained a typed collection of poems. The first few described their writer taking a walk in the country, with lots of detail about trees, hedges, sky, views of hills and so on. They weren't bad, actually. Then the poems' writer described finding dead animals — rabbits caught in traps, pheasants mangled by shot. As I turned the pages, I knew what was coming. The last pieces in the series described me. The physical details were quite accurate, suggesting that their writer must have had access to my photograph. I was also trapped and mangled, with the difference that I was not dead.

My agent said we should take the poems to the police. Eventually I was informed that their author was serving a sentence for 'serious sex crimes' in a maximum-security prison in the West Country. I was not permitted to know the writer's name, or what offence he had committed, but I was assured that 'measures would be taken'. That was all. I had always wondered if, one day, the man would be released, and that I would open the front door to find him standing there with a knife in his hand. What 'measures' could be taken against that eventuality I had no idea.

Sebastian had a whole troop of groupies who sometimes waited outside his house in Soho. One of them had managed to get into the hallway, where she spent the night on the floor, howling like a dog because Sebastian didn't love her as she loved him. He made her a cup of tea, which for him was an act of rare kindness, and called an ambulance. Perhaps she might have felt better had she known of his aversion to food and drink. I made a joke of the sex-offender poems to Sebastian, suggesting that I had a better class of stalker, someone who had shown a real degree of commitment.

If Anne Clarke was a he after all, could it be the sadistic nature poet? There had been no handwriting on the sheaf of poems and besides they had presumably been thrown away long ago. If I printed out the emails and took them to the police with the card, what would they say? By whom had I reason to suspect they had been sent? If it wasn't the poet who fantasised so graphically about eviscerating me, that left me back with my lovers' wives. If the police went to their homes to ask questions, then two out of the three women would receive an extremely unpleasant shock. Not only would they discover their husband had been having an affair, but they would be involved in a police investigation. *Oh*, I thought, *Anne Clarke, you have been very clever.* So, I did nothing.

That evening I helped my daughter build a cardboard model of a sinkhole for her school geography project, I threw some ravioli in a pan for her supper and after she was asleep, I double locked the door and selected a sleeping pill. After Sebastian's death I had had a prescription for Zopiclone from the GP to get me through the first weeks of mourning. Zopis are the queen of sleeping pills. Unlike the gentle woolly blur of Valium, or Alazopram which teases you softly under in stages, Zopiclone is like a blind rattling down on your mind. Oblivion guaranteed, delivered to your door from convenient illegal website *britishsleepingpills.co.uk*. The name changes every few weeks but they're very reliable. That night I settled for an over-the-counter Sominex, lest Anne Clarke was still creeping around.

The next morning, I bought a security chain from Mr Ali's hardware shop round the corner, and from then on kept it in place whenever I was in the flat.

*

Mr Ali was a refugee from Iraq. Before coming to England, he had been a theatre director who specialised in Shakespeare, making his own translations into Arabic for his productions. I never knew quite how to speak to Mr Ali. Part of me thought that he might enjoy discussing Shakespeare, but I worried that it would appear condescending of me to try to engage him in conversation. Perhaps it would upset him to recall his past life, now that he had to wear a black and red sweatshirt with the name of the hardware shop on it. I wanted him to know that I could see past the sweatshirt, but why would he care if I did? Why would Mr Ali give a flying fuck for my opinion on *A Midsummer Night's Dream* when Tony Blair had blown up his house and his theatre and he was living with his wife and three children in two rooms above a London hardware shop? What right did I have to assuage my middle-class guilt with a few comments about *Macbeth*?

Once I had bought two tickets for *Antony and Cleopatra* at the Globe and taken them round to him in an envelope. I pretended that I had been sent them as a gift from a paper I reviewed for, but I was going to be out of town that day. Might Mr Ali be able to use them?

'Perhaps your wife might enjoy it?' I asked, too eagerly.

The Globe was also performing *Titus Andronicus*, but apparently it was a very violent staging, which hadn't seemed tactful. I didn't know Mrs Ali's name and it seemed disrespectful to ask. Afterwards Mr Ali told me that sadly his wife had been unable to attend, but he had enjoyed the show very much. We had a long talk about it, yet afterwards I could have kicked myself. Of course Mrs Ali couldn't go, a babysitter was probably an unaffordable luxury. Mr Ali made me feel ashamed in so many ways that following *Antony and Cleopatra* I usually asked a few polite questions and then 'forgot' the change from whatever I had purchased, after which I could feel ashamed about that, too.

*

Anne's postcard had flipped our positions. She wanted to shock me, to show that she could observe me if she chose to. I thought that she had probably made her point and that it was unlikely I would hear from her again. Several writers I knew had received much stranger things in the post than poems or cards, not necessarily sinister. A historical novelist I sometimes chatted to at the London Library had once been sent a Dyson vacuum cleaner by a reader who had seen an interview with her in her home. The accompanying note explained that her curtains looked dusty and included instructions of which attachment to use to clean them. If you publish books or articles, people make all sorts of assumptions about you. They put photos of your shoes on Wikifeet and in the comments below the line they write that it's no wonder you can't keep a man because you look like a weasel.

However, the black notebook from Sicily was filling up. Working out who Anne might be began to fascinate me. Writing about Emma, Polly and Lucy had become my new evening ritual. After my daughter was in bed, I would clean up the kitchen and give a wipe to the table where I wrote. Tuning the radio to Classic FM or Radio 3, I poured myself a glass of wine (at the time I allowed myself two, one before and one after dinner), set out the notebook with the edge carefully in parallel to the tabletop, uncapped my fountain pen, lit a cigarette and began.

My literary agent was dunning me for work. He thought I should be producing a thriller, something twisty and exciting which transformed a downtrodden woman into an unlikely heroine in a dangerous part of the world. I had researched several such stories and written up proposals and opening chapters, but my agent had been unable to sell them, mainly because they were lousy. Instead, I typed up a proposal based on the memories and observations I had set down in the black notebook. I was curious about the idea of writing a novel based on Lucy, Emma and Polly and how their lives had become entwined with my own. My agent was not happy. He wanted to know why I thought anyone would be interested in reading about my lovers' wives. What about the moral implications? Why did I want to expose myself as an adulterous woman?

He was also disgusted by the passage I had written about shitting. It was 'unnecessary" and 'unseemly'. He might as well have said 'unladylike'. What about *Ulysses*, I countered? Not that I was comparing myself to James Joyce, but what about Leopold Bloom sitting on the loo reading a magazine, complacently examining his evacuation and wiping his bottom with a short story called 'Matcham's Masterstroke'? Jonathan Swift's magnificently scathing scatology? What about Erica Jong's digression on the connection between toilet bowls and national character in *Fear of Flying*? The symbolic distribution of lavatory paper at the end of *The Balkan Trilogy*? I got quite carried away, trying to think of all the examples I could remember of well-known writers who had mentioned shit.

My agent changed tack. He advised me that it was unwise to write about drinking. There had been a brief fashion for books about women who boozed and took pills, but the female narrator whose unreliability is down to the fact that she's off her tits had already become a cliché. I said I was interested that whilst male writers have a long and undignified history of describing alcohol — Hemingway, for example, or Norman Mailer — the subject for women had gone from transgressive to trite in a couple of years. No one reads Norman Mailer now, said my agent. What about Edward St Aubyn then? He'd built his whole career on the desperate poetry of drink and drugs. Altogether, you could barely move in bookshops for heroic men struggling with their addictions. Whatever, said my agent, the theme had been done as far as women were concerned and it wouldn't sell.

A few hours after our conversation he emailed me: 'You should be careful,' he wrote. 'This reads as the work of someone who is bitter and damaged.'

Well, I thought. *Well, yes.*

I continued writing in the black notebook.

5. EXPENSES

F came into the kitchen when I was inserting the point of a carving knife into the shell of a quail's egg. He picked another knife from the block and began to help me; he knew just what to do. You have to prise apart the pale blue shell just enough to pour the egg out whole into the *croustade*, in which there is already a sliver of summer truffle, then add a quarter- teaspoon of double cream and a grate of black pepper before baking in the oven at 180 degrees for ten minutes, so the egg is just set. Sprinkle with dill to serve. It sounds a pretentious thing to be making for a weekday dinner but as I lived in the Swedish district of London (opposite the Swedish Church, just along from the Swedish pub, round the corner from the Swedish Embassy which was next to the Swedish grocers), the ingredients were easy to come by as apparently quails' eggs are not considered too fancy in Sweden. Still, it's a slippery, fiddly job and I was impressed that F took to it so smoothly.

The dinner seemed to go quite well. F made several references to the time he spent 'single-dadding'. Some of my guests were parents, some were not, but I noticed that all the women at the table responded warmly to this phrase, nodding empathetically as F described taking his children away for the weekend alone. Over pudding, people were talking about the places they dreamed of living if they could escape from London. I said I wanted to live in a small, old city near the sea — Tangier or maybe Mahon or Venice. F agreed that it would be a dream to live in Tangier.

*

F told me about Polly the following week, at dinner in a French restaurant after we had been to a play together. He set both his hands on the tablecloth and stared at them for some time. Then he raised his head slowly until his eyes met mine.

'I have a wife.'

When men state this fact so explicitly, it is one of two reasons, the first being obviously that they want it to be clear that they are "taken". The second is tantamount to an invitation.

"You said you were a single father", I replied.

F explained that Polly had changed career and was retraining as a counsellor. This sometimes required her to be away from home on residential courses, hence the time spent 'single- dadding'. I pointed out that looking after your own children was not babysitting, or remotely akin to being a lone parent. F looked momentarily irritated, then I watched him consciously smooth out his face. He claimed to feel a lone parent because Polly never took any interest in his work, never read a word he wrote. She did not like socialising or literary parties, she preferred to stay at home, which was very difficult for F as he was convinced (or it suited him to believe), that going to events and being visible was important to his career. He had never mentioned that he was married, he said, because he and his wife had an 'understanding'. Polly appreciated that unconventional arrangements were usual 'in the arts'. F said he wanted to be honest with me, that he would never divorce because of the children and needed to be clear about that. None of this was at all surprising, though it staggers me, absolutely baffles and confounds me, that I didn't leave as soon as he said 'in the arts'. How could you want to fuck anyone who talked about themselves like that? I did though. I got right on with it in the taxi back to my place.

*

I got to hear a lot about how unsympathetic Polly was to F's ambitions, he got terribly worked up about it. Once, in an East End hotel, I dozed off while he was going on about how he suffered, but he didn't notice. I didn't really listen when he started lamenting; I thought of his complaints as a kind of 'cock tax'. This was a phrase used by H and his friends. Cock tax was the amount of rubbish you had to listen to a woman talking before you could have sex with her, but it seemed to apply just as well the other way round.

*

The grumbling was tedious, but I couldn't deny that it was also flattering. F complimented me at Polly's expense and I craved the comparisons. With F, I felt beautiful, clever, understood, valued. However late we stayed up drinking and chatting the world felt bright and thrilling in the morning, he gave me back an energy I had thought lost, a belief in possibility, a new relish and pleasure in talking and thinking. Like all new lovers, we made a closed world that we believed no one else had the key to, and even if we were both too old to know it as fresh magic, we believed in it none the less.

I began to accompany F to book launches and prize parties when I could. In so far as anyone was interested, I felt that we were accepted as a couple. I introduced F to my friends and they began to invite us together with no one saying a word about Polly's existence, though F continued to speak about his children openly. Since F's family home was far from central London, he had a series of floating arrangements — borrowed flats belonging to various friends -- where he would spend several nights each week, though often he stayed with me, arriving after my daughter had gone to bed and leaving very early, before I had to get her up for school. I took this as confirmation of his arrangement with Polly.

Our relationship had been going on for some months when F had a new book out. His publishers arranged the usual launch event, which consisted of standing around in a bookshop drinking the notoriously nasty white wine provided at such things while F signed copies and received congratulations. I went to the party with him instead of Polly and we continued to a small dinner in the private dining room of the Royal Academy. Something had gone wrong with the heating and the room was freezing. It was so cold that the Bearnaise sauce served on top of the beef tournedos had set in solid coins. Everyone pretended not to notice, but the dinner was not a success, particularly for the women who were shivering in their cocktail dresses. F gave me his suit jacket to put over my shoulders. Before we left, I went to the loo and as I was hunched over to pee, clutching my elbows for warmth, I felt something against my knee. In the inside breast pocket of F's jacket was a card with an Art-Deco drawing of a peacock on it. Inside, Polly had written a long note — about how proud she was of F, how she rejoiced that their conversations resonated in every word he wrote and how sorry she was that she could not be by his side at the launch but that she was present with him every moment. And there I'd been, tripping around on his arm like fucking Juliet.

The irony of our reversed positions was not lost on me. Polly wrote as the plaintive mistress, the 'secret friend' who can't be acknowledged in public, whilst I played the shocked and wounded wife. As sensible spouses do, I kept my discovery to myself while I prepared my attack.

*

At the beginning of his novel *Inside Story*, Martin Amis apologises disingenuously to his readers for all the name-dropping. Disingenuously because he has in fact changed several names of real people: his wife, his daughter. But he keeps 'my friend Salman', 'my friend Zadie'. What he doesn't seem to have twigged is that there is no apology required, since most people (unless they are readers of Martin Amis) neither know or care who 'Salman' and 'Zadie' are. He might as well be talking about his cats.

Amis then describes a scene at his daughter's primary school in Cobble Hill, Brooklyn, where after giving a talk he asks the class how many of them want to become writers. Two thirds of the pupils raise their hands, which Amis concludes as being evidence that 'the urge to write is universal'. He does not consider that writing is an ideal occupation for the humanistically educated children of the global upper classes whose labour has become irrelevant to capitalism. Between the techies and the drones there's a small but distinct class of people whose practical engagement the system no longer needs. A miniature industry has grown up to service their urge to express themselves — the MFA programmes, the creative writing retreats, the niche magazines -- participation in all of which is a perfectly pleasant way to pass one's time so long as one's parents are paying the rent on the studio in Berlin or the loft in Red Hook. The other option is becoming an artist; either way, Amis's 'universal urge to write' might be better described as the urge to produce Shit That Wouldn't Exist Unless Your Dad Is Rich.

*

My affair with F coincided with the moment that publishers began to insist that their authors use social media. Whether people who liked to spend their time looking at other people's breakfasts or holidays actually bought books was not the point. Scrambling desperately late to the party, the new digital divisions of the big publishing houses urged writers to accumulate followers and likes; everyone had to be on Instagram and Twitter, so my colleagues were duly posting and engaging and, in some cases, attracting several hundred followers. The day after I found the card I started snooping online into Polly's life, but I didn't get very far with either her married or her maiden name. Neither of us were on Facebook, whilst F's Wikipedia page made no mention of family. There was one black and white photograph on the alumni site of Polly's old university, but it was about thirty years old. In that picture Polly had long hair, wide-set, clear eyes and a beauty spot high on her right cheekbone, like an actress in a Restoration comedy.

I had an Instagram account too but I seldom posted anything. Every now and then I remembered that I was supposed to be 'active online' and spent a few monkeyish minutes stabbing 'like' at the benign, effortful communications of the few people who followed me, without bothering to read the captions. Now I called up F's account and went through it carefully. He seemed pretty keen, diligently puffing colleagues' work and commenting on politics, but it was all impersonal, I discovered nothing I didn't know.

*

Just as their manner of going about infidelity indicated their places in the class system, so too did the rooms where H, B and F wrote. Their studies were inversely proportional to their respective status anxieties.

H's study, where Lucy might have slipped on his cum, was the most unassuming space in an otherwise rather grand house, small and practical.

B wrote at a huge double "partner" desk in the wing of his home reserved for guests. One wall was filled with copies of his books in all their various editions and translations and another with framed photographs of him receiving awards and attending prestigious conferences and festivals.

I never went to F's house, but I knew that it was the largest of all, a huge ramshackle Victorian pile in one of the London suburbs that are always described as 'leafy' which he and Polly were gradually restoring. F's study was referred to as the Library and it took up half of the first floor. He described its large bay windows, the antique daybed with velvet cover (on which he claimed he frequently spent the night, as of course he and Polly didn't sleep together), and the walls, which were painted in Farrow and Ball's 'Book Room Red'. The Library also featured three pairs of stags' antlers mounted over the fireplace.

In fact, F didn't need to describe the Library to me as I had had a good look at it online. When Polly went away for her courses, F would take the children on his 'single-dadding' weekends so that the house could be let on AirBnB. Given the size of the house and its position on the edge of town it was particularly profitable during Ascot week, when F told me they often rented to people who had tickets to the Royal Enclosure. One of the Royal Enclosure guests had written on the site that the decoration of the house made it resemble a private members' club, which I did not consider to be an apex compliment.

I had never had a study. All my books and articles had been written at kitchen tables. In the various flats we lived in during our time together, my husband had had a studio, or at least a desk, because as a musician he needed silence more than I did. Naturally I felt extremely resentful about this but I had enjoyed and nurtured the emotion as it made me feel secretly superior and agreeably martyred at the same time. I made my work incidental, something to be put aside when it was time to cook supper. Whilst this became one of the many poisons that crept ineluctably through our marriage there was no doubt I had done it to myself.

*

It was F's study which led me to what he had been hiding about Polly. I found a picture taken at a summer lunch in what was evidently F's garden. He had described the white wrought-iron porch which stood out over the terrace beneath the bay window of the first-floor Library, a corner of which was visible in the snap. A group of people gathered round the table all smiling at the camera, holding up glasses in a toast. Diagonal to the lacy ironwork at the top left was a foot in a Birkenstock sandal, attached to a leg which poked out from under a long flower-printed skirt and a baggy tunic top. It was hard to see the face of the woman wearing these clothes, but I magnified the picture and spun it and stared and there it was, the birthmark on the cheekbone. The eyes were deeper set and the birthmark looked much farther away than in the university picture, because Polly was fat. Polly was obese.

The black notebook was ruthless. I had set myself the task of recording what I knew and thought about my lovers' wives. There was no getting around it. Writing the word in slow cursive on a fresh line didn't make it any better. What did I think when I discovered the picture of Polly?

Good.

'IS YOUR MAN A CHEATER? HOW TO SPOT THE SIGNS!'

A version of this article must have been published every day for the last fifty years. Practically every woman in Europe must have read it at least once. We all know the signals, the clues to look for, but none of the hundreds of versions I had absorbed myself included kindness as a sign that your husband or boyfriend was 'playing away'.

Unexpected bunches of crumpled supermarket flowers, yes; suggesting a long country walk where you can talk freely about your feelings without being interrupted, no. In a lengthy affair, the wife's worries, her hormonal patterns, her difficulties with the teenage children or the sibling who won't pull their weight with the aged parents all become topics for discussion. The hidden woman, the secret friend, the mistress, will treat her lover's marital frustrations with soothing sympathy. She will listen, she will be wise, she will *understand*. Gently, she will advocate for the wife, persuading her lover that he needs to see things from her point of view. Women, explains the mistress, need to be cherished, supported, above all, listened to. It's the small, loving gestures that make the difference.

So if your husband tells you to have an extra hour in bed while he takes the kids to football practice, if he books a surprise spa weekend for you and your best friend because you need some 'me time', if he offers to drive your mother to the retail park and spend three hours helping her choose a new fridge, there's a good chance he's got a secret.

*

One of the things I discussed frequently with F was money. People assume that published writers, especially if they appear on the television or in broadsheet newspapers, must be rich, or at least paying the bills without too much trouble. Certainly, some globally successful authors can command huge advances and book-to-film adaptions pay well, but the publishing industry had been haemorrhaging profit for twenty years, at the same time as the field is becoming ever more crowded. H had family money as well as what he earned from his books, B had been hugely successful before the bottom fell out of the market, but F was like me. Unlike many artists and writers we really did live on what we earned and it was never, ever enough. We grumbled together about the endless days of unpaid work we were expected to do, about the casual tardiness with which publishers who insisted on deadlines being met to the contractual letter then took months to pay, about the free copy we were expected to provide for magazines in exchange for a one-line mention of our books at the bottom of the page. We calculated that even on a book advance of £100,000 — a juicy figure and not so usual nowadays — by the time you had knocked off fifteen per cent for the agent and divided the remaining £85,000 over the three years it took to deliver the book, you would be earning approximately £28,000 per year before tax. Not minimum wage, true, but below the national average.

To be able to be frank with F about my financial anxieties was a relief. Writing books professionally was still glossed as the pursuit of the liberal amateur, the artist or intellectual who was above such vulgarities as paying the electricity bill. Discussing money in publishing was viewed as *infra dig* (that's what agents were for, to protect their authors' sensibilities), so confessing to our worries and frustrations, to the humiliations exacted by living from cheque to cheque was comforting for us both. F knew what it felt like to go a week with £5.37 in the current account, no savings and the credit card maxed. He was familiar with the obsequious, Dickensian emails I was always sending, respectfully drawing attention to the outstanding payment for work I had delivered weeks before, with the schizophrenic feeling engendered by invitations to smart events where you were supposed to push your career whilst knowing you'd have to walk home afterwards in the cold because you didn't have the bus fare. F's life looked prosperous from the outside, as perhaps did mine, but admitting, at least to one another, that it was a game of spillikins where one loose straw could send everything crashing down was a great solace.

Given my circumstances, F thought it was somewhat absurd for me to send my daughter to a private all-girls school. He suggested this might be to do with my own status anxieties. Unlike F, I didn't own a house or a car or even a television; apart from books, I had almost no possessions. The fees for the school ate nearly everything I earned; I was frequently behind with the rent and my landlady retaliated by refusing to fix things when they went wrong in the flat. Once we had gone a whole winter without heating. I wasn't poor, of course I wasn't poor, but my life always felt precarious.

No one was working twelve-hour shifts as a cleaner in a factory, no one had to wear a uniform or ask if the customer wanted fries. We knew that our freedom to order our days, to spend our time reading and thinking was a vast privilege, but in exchange we had renounced certain things. We had exchanged the prospect of security for perennially deferred hope, the regular salary and the pension plan for a specious prestige that no one beyond a minute circle any longer believed was relevant or worthwhile.

In the rich parts of the world where acquiring and reading books was even a possibility, they had lost all function in the majority of people's lives. When my parents had moved into the house where I spent most of my childhood, one of the removal men had said to my mother: 'You've got fuck all else, Missus, but you've got a lot of books!' People are no longer ashamed to live in bookless houses, but to my parents' generation books were a sign of education and status. My parents read their books, whilst many of the people they knew probably didn't, but to have shelves filled with books, rather than untouched china ornaments, declared that you had joined the middle classes.

For F and me, the pros, those who however inadequate our efforts are none the less trying to live on them, it's a zero-sum game. Once upon a time the Booker Prize was shown live on television, soon it will be as risible an accolade as Hair Colourist of the year. Greasy-faced authors in rented dinner jackets will assemble self-importantly in the banqueting suites of declining hotels to talk over the speeches and applaud the awarding of a lump of plastic which no one outside the trade gives a toss about.

However it seems, books have mostly had their future. F and I were no better than handloom weavers, but it was the only job we had ever done or knew how to do and our mutual self-pity was as gratifying for us to talk about as it was pathetic to listen to. Where we differed was that F still believed he could 'make it'. He wanted to be wealthy and well known, he wanted the world to validate him as well as pay him, whereas I had no such ambition. I wanted not to feel relieved when the ATM made the whirring noise that meant it was delivering the cash, but when I told him he didn't believe me.

*

One evening we were sitting on the kerb in Soho Square. We could have taken a bench in the garden but the kerb seemed like a good place, probably because we were both rather drunk. We had been having our money conversation again. F was talking about the mortgage payments on his house on the edge of town.

'She just doesn't understand. She keeps on spending. .'

'Polly?'

'Who else?'

F had his head in his hands. It came out that they had recently remortgaged the house in order to pay for refitting the kitchen. Polly had been using the fresh capital to pay for her counselling course. This seemed reasonable enough, I ventured, as it was an investment in her future career. F thought it was selfish.

'She won't even think about working. She says she's too busy with the children. And the supermarket bills . . .'

'What?'

Whilst clearing out the kitchen to get ready for the builders, F had found caches of expensive food and vintage wine. Polly had become a sort of upscale prepper — when the zombie apocalypse came F's family would be eating a lot of truffles hunkered down in the shed. She was squirrelling away twenty-pound jars of Manuka honey, lavender-scented chocolates, artful glass bottles of Umbrian porcini essence, boxes and boxes of organic shortbread in a wide variety of flavours. Underneath the chicken breasts and Tupperware containers of stew in the chest freezer, F discovered whole beef fillets, breasts of grouse and a turbot with accompanying sachet of ready-made champagne shallot sauce. F confronted her and she confessed to having spent thousands of pounds. How could she possibly have been so irrational, so irresponsible?

'Well, she's obviously angry.'

'What does she have to be angry about?'

I took a deep breath. 'Polly's been eating her pain for years. She's obviously in agony. You're ashamed of her, because she's fat. That's why you don't go out with her, why you spend half your time away from home, because it doesn't suit the way you want to project yourself, to have a fat wife. She's not stupid. You told me she understands that infidelity is usual "in the arts", but that's crap. She's angry and she's punishing you because somehow you've done this to her. You're prancing round town with me and whoever else and she's at home with the family-sized Cadbury's Wholenut. You refused to look at that, so she's upped the ante.'

F got to his feet, somewhat unsteadily, 'I can't believe you're being such a bitch.'

'Bitch is what men call women when they tell the truth. Why don't you ask Polly why she's spunked the new Aga on artisan crisps? Perhaps she can write her answer on a postcard with a peacock on it.'

'I'm leaving.'

'OK. You can put one of us out of our misery. Your call.'

I was not to see F again for over a year.

6. ON THE CIRCUIT

I was far less curious about Lucy than Polly, but then I didn't have to be. I knew what brand of laundry liquid she used, the colours of her sofas, the timbre of the street-sounds that could be heard from her home at different times of day. And of course I had met, or rather encountered, her several times. Lucy had given up her staff job on a national newspaper when her first child was born, but she continued to work as a freelance health journalist. She had a chemistry degree, but she mostly wrote for what editors had only recently ceased to call the 'women's pages' — articles about nutrition, diet, exercise or the relative benefits of the latest super-ingredients in beauty products.

The closest I had come to Lucy was at a literary festival in the Georgian spa town of Buxton in Derbyshire. I had been invited to take part in a panel discussion of the importance of fashion in history, whilst she was commenting on the use of poison in famous novels. H said Lucy enjoyed being asked to speak at festivals; she was confident on the platform and it made her feel 'part of things'. Sometimes they attended the festivals together.

Going to literary festivals was very much part of my job so I tried to be professional about it. People had paid to hear me speak and they deserved to be entertained. Festivals had bloomed all over the country and writers had responded, producing slick, dramatic talks, with carefully timed jokes and impressive Power-Point presentations which I did my best to imitate, though it was beyond me why anyone would want to go to such things. I spent most of my life reading, but I had never felt the least desire to meet an author, even Jane Austen or Michel Houellebecq. Even reading a biography of a writer I admired felt unnecessarily nosy and intrusive. I was once asked in one of those newspaper questionnaires which writers I would invite to a fantasy dinner party, but I couldn't honestly think of a single one. Even in my imagination they would be disappointed in me and I in them and it was an altogether dreadful idea, though naturally I claimed to the newspaper that I would love to dine with Proust and Evelyn Waugh.

My mother came with me to the Buxton festival as I thought that once I'd got the event out of the way we could spend an afternoon walking in the countryside. The speakers were all staying in the same hotel and when my mother and I arrived there the evening before the festival the first person I saw was Lucy, walking down the impressive carved staircase towards me. We nodded and said hello as she walked across the lobby past the check-in desk.

'Isn't that lady beautifully made up?' observed my mother.

Later we went to dinner and there was Lucy, sitting with three other women in the restaurant. I knew one of them so I had to go and say good evening. She introduced me briefly to the other two and asked if I knew Lucy. We said hello again and made a few remarks about the last festivals we had been to.

'I'm looking forward to your talk,' said my mother politely to Lucy.

'We should let you carry on with your evening,' I said quickly in what I hoped was a light and social tone. I didn't want my mother getting into conversation, so I led her to a corner table away from Lucy and her friends. We both ordered the seafood stew.

'Rather you than me,' said the waitress. 'You couldn't pay me to eat that.'

I could hear my phone vibrating in my handbag. It was H,

texting me. He knew that Lucy and I were both in Buxton and he thought it was amusing.

The festival events were taking place in a modern annexe connected to the main hotel by a glassed-in corridor. While the audience took their seats, I stood with the three other speakers to be fitted with a microphone headset, lifting my chin to the greygreen view of the Derbyshire hills while the technician fiddled to clip the battery pack to my waistband.

'Will we really need these?' I asked him. 'I can't imagine there'll be so many people.'

'Makes no difference anyway,' the technician said cheerfully. 'They're all deaf.'

The large room was chilly and smelled faintly of gravy. Lucy was sitting in the middle of the front row, just a couple of metres away from the low stage. As my mother had noticed, she was, as always, 'beautifully made up'; not with heavy foundation or garish lipstick, but the full complement of eyeliner, shadow, blush, eyebrow pencil and powder subtly and painstakingly applied. Lucy was a more conservative dresser than Emma, much less stylish to be truthful, but she loved pretty shoes, of which she had a huge collection. They were kept carefully in their boxes in a special wardrobe, their toes padded with tissue paper. Today she was wearing charcoal-grey suede pumps a shade darker than her skirt, with a trim of fuchsia grosgrain ribbon on the heel seam.

As the lights went down, I saw the diamond in Lucy's engagement ring glinting. While the chair of the discussion was making the introductions, I thought of H telling me how he had proposed to her with that ring on her thirtieth birthday. It came from the same shop in the Burlington Arcade as a birthday present he had given to me: the doublestranded diamond tennis bracelet that I was wearing on my right wrist. I thought of how Lucy was particular about her hair — she would never let H have the car window open when they went out in the evening lest she arrived looking dishevelled. I thought that I had recently taken part in a threesome with her husband and a Russian prostitute in her bed, of the shampoo she favoured, of the quarrel she and H had recently had about the cost of redecorating their bathroom. H had grown up with chilly, Spartan, English bathrooms and thought it a waste of money to install underfloor heating and a double shower, but Lucy had got her way. I wondered what would happen if I leant forward until the light in our diamonds mingled, to tell her that I was on her side, that given how much time women have to spend in the bathroom comfort should never be neglected, but then the chairperson turned to me and asked if I would like to open the discussion with a comment on the way in which Eleanor of Aquitaine had manipulated dress to enforce her power.

As a professional, Lucy left the room before the closing questions. This part of literary festivals is even worse than having to give the talk. Most 'questions' tend to be put by people excited at the chance to get a microphone in their grip and offer their own opinions, often on topics entirely unrelated to the discussion in hand.

After that business, the waitress from the restaurant came up to me with a copy of my first book to sign. 'I got it in Oxfam,' she explained. 'Can't say I bothered with it really, but I thought I might as well bring it.'

Later, H told me that Lucy had enjoyed the talk. He was quite tickled by her comment that what I said had been interesting. It had surprised Fragrant Lucy that I had any opinions about medieval conceptions of *magnificenza*, because up until then she had thought of me as 'that woman who writes about sex'.

*

Saul Bellow, in *Augie March*, describes a writer's work thus: 'All the while you thought you were going around idle terribly hard work was taking place. Hard, hard work, excavation and digging, mining, moling through tunnels, heaving, pushing, moving rock, working, working, working, working, panting, hawling, hoisting. And none of this work is seen from the outside.'

It is necessary to be interested in the idea of America to appreciate Saul Bellow; or at least to believe that Donald Trump is an aberration rather than an obvious conclusion. I wasn't and didn't, but I had copied this quote into a notebook as an example of risible masculine conceit.

*

Something else Lucy had in common with Emma and Polly — apart from me — was the reverence with which she treated her husband's career. With apparent sincerity, all three bought into the idea that being a writer was something sacred, fussing round their great men in their respective studies, ensuring that the home ran smoothly with minimum disturbance to The Important Work in Progress. H told me that his only domestic skill was preparing scrambled eggs on toast. He had never made a cup of tea or coffee, never changed a duvet cover or a nappy or mopped a floor or scrubbed his own piss from the underside of the lavatory seat. He and Lucy had a lot of help, but still, I asked him, who put the laundry on at weekends?

'She does.'

'Why? Because she's got a vagina?'

H was unrepentant. It wasn't that he thought he was clever for having avoided any form of housework in fifty odd years, he hadn't even got as far as conceiving of it as something that might involve him. I tried to explain to him how much of Lucy's time, how many increments of minutes were taken up by such tasks, not only the time occupied by executing them, but in thinking and planning all the logistics of running a household.

'So what's your excuse then?'

'For not doing the laundry?'

'No, for not winning the Nobel Prize?'

*

B took his children to school and claimed to be an excellent cook. He had prepared dinner when he first married Emma, but she made him stop as his food was so delicious she was putting on weight. He was considerably more engaged at home than H, yet still acted as though anything he did outside writing was a concession for which he deserved praise. B was also fond of prefacing remarks with the phrase 'Speaking as a writer . . .', as though he bore some mystic burden. His daily round at home consisted of the school run followed by the day at his desk before dinner with the family and an evening in front of the television, yet when I asked him how things had gone, he never failed to say 'another day at the coal face'.

F was even more irritating than B when it came to quarrying his little heart out. When he was in London he liked to work in cafés. Many people do so out of choice as well as necessity, though in F's case I always thought he was terribly keen to be seen doing it. 'Look at me! I'm a Writer! See me tapping on my laptop. Watch as I artfully consider the placing of a comma!' That didn't stop him from informing me that he was 'off to pretend to be a writer' or had spent the afternoon 'pretending to be a writer'. Do plumbers say they are 'pretending' when they fix their customers' boilers? Do surgeons say, 'Just off to pretend to do a kidney transplant.' as they leave for the hospital? Why should writing be seen as so sacred that even approaching it in a practical fashion needs to be guarded with false modesty? The implication is that writing is so marvellous, so otherworldly, that it needs to be spoken of with faux humility, not because it's unimportant but because it's so extraordinary, such an exceptional thing to be doing that you wouldn't want ordinary civilians to think you were up yourself. Which you are.

Perhaps I was just jealous of my lovers' ability to take themselves seriously, not to mention of the wives who cossetted their talents and treated them with such respect. Virginia Woolf is mostly a writer who makes me want to spit, not least because of her endlessly recycled quote: 'A woman must have money and a room of her own if she is to write.' It is men who require the sanctum, the tiptoeing on the landing outside the study door, the reverent attention to the tap of the keyboard.

7. BLONDE VENUS

Lucy had a point about me. Whatever else I did, the editors who asked me to write features more often than not wanted them to be about sex. When my first book had been published in my twenties, this had seemed like a choice. Later, and partly because of Sebastian, it became an association from which I could not escape.

In 1999, an historian named Amanda Foreman took part in a photo shoot for *Tatler* magazine in which she was posed apparently naked behind a pile of books, her biography of Georgiana, Duchess of Devonshire. The picture was reprinted in all the British newspapers and became the topic of much debate. At the time, clever women were not expected to behave in such a fashion. Was it empowering or anti-feminist to have publicised a book in this manner? Was it 'legitimate' for a scholar to promote a history in her bare skin? Quite who was supposed to determine the legitimacy of Dr Foreman's choice was seldom investigated, but what bewildered many of the commentators at the time was that a brilliantly intelligent woman would take her clothes off in public. Subversive satire, or pandering to the patriarchy?

*

By the time my own first biography came out, about Athenais de Montespan and her lover Louis XIV, publishers actively encouraged their female writers to do 'sexy" shoots. *Georgiana* had been a huge commercial success and the houses were looking for the 'next Amanda Foreman'. Since the subject of my book had been a royal mistress, I proposed a feature for the *Tatler* on 'mistress know-how' a list of do's and don'ts for aspiring adulteresses. It included advice such as, 'Men may come and men may go but Vuitton lasts for ever. Get durables.' Other suggestions were related to shoes — 'Warty-heeled Tod's are for wives' — and conversational topics to avoid, 'Don't discuss your gluten allergy, or your daddy issues.' It was meant to be tongue-in-cheek, worldly and knowing. The advice was repellently servile but, as I would come to learn, pretty sound. For the picture which accompanied it I wore a leopard-print coat, fishnet stockings and high black patent leather boots. I looked like a hard-faced comedy barmaid.

*

One consequence of F calling me a bitch in Soho Square was that things picked up on the financial front. F broke off all contact for about a year, during which time I met B. My historian friend Cathryn had bought tickets for a 'literary dinner' at a restaurant quite near where I lived. It was part of a series of such events, and several writers I knew had already done them. The lady who organised the literary dinners was much cannier than the organisers of most festivals. Her restaurant was enchanting, on a quiet corner just off Baker Street, filled with flowers and fairy lights and unusual old pictures. The guest writers were instructed to speak very briefly between the courses of the dinner, which was amusingly tailored to the theme of their books. If they droned on too long, they were interrupted by the waiters firmly setting down the plates. The food was always delicious and the owner made sure that it was accompanied by plenty of wine.

B was a friend of the speaker, a poet, and we found ourselves seated at the same table. His taste in clothes was awful but otherwise he had potential. He was much better looking than either F or H, a noticeably attractive man, though I did observe that he seemed uneasy after his friend's talk, anxious to let everyone know that he too was a well-known writer. He tried to impress the company by telling them about how much money he had made from his books, several of which had been made into films. When I went outside to smoke, he followed me and asked for a cigarette, though I later learned that he hated smoking. B wrote detective novels, so we talked for a while about his favourite authors, including Raymond Chandler. I had written a piece on Chandler and offered to email it to him. We exchanged details.

*

The article I emailed to B the next morning was titled 'Marlowe's Blondes'. It discussed the luscious, corrupted women favoured by Chandler's noir detective Philip Marlowe. The third paragraph went:

"Florian's has become a gambling joint in downtown Hollywood rather than an oasis of calm in the Piazza St Marco, the drink-sodden aristocracy of Hollywood inhabit faux-baronial mansions, and Marlowe keeps the faith with French coffee and the French defence. He may quote T.S. Eliot, but the homecoming queens of his cornfed childhood have become two-bit hustlers wearing nothing beneath their drum majorette's shakos but glazed hessian boots, and the wasteland is where he belongs. Chandler's America figures as the kind of whorish girl Marlowe, despite himself, desires. Despite her acid smogs and her bad grammar, despite her TV habit, evil food and obsession with consumption, whatever you need, wherever you happen to be, she'll have it. Somewhere out there is God's own country, but in his darker moments Marlowe has to admit that it doesn't interest him all that much."

B had told me enough about himself to make it clear that his self image was the type of man who might tilt his fedora from his brow with the barrel of his Colt, a man whose cynicism was predicate on his purity. His silver belt buckle identified him as the disillusioned descendant of the original urban cowboy, who likes his girls "hard-boiled and loaded with sin". In case he missed the point, I added a line:

"Chandler's Los Angeles may be the brothel of America's soul, but he is under no illusions as to the desert of marriage à la midwest. The conjugal kitchen may be bright white and shiny, but the marital bed is as cold as the brand new icebox."

I was pretty sure the words would do the trick and I was right. B asked me to lunch with him the following week.

*

According to B, Emma was definitely not a 'sex woman'. Once I'd got to know him better, I thought I could see why. In one of his text messages to me, B wrote: 'I thought I was finished as a man until I met you.' What had happened to B, what despite his lifetime of extra-marital encounters he was unable to accept, was that he was growing impotent.

B insisted that Emma's lack of interest in sex was behind his infidelity to her. I knew about the Dutch book publicist, the Italian publishing assistant, the American fixer. I knew about the successful magazine editor, who had been given the diamond pendant. Emma knew the editor too — at least she knew her well enough to have asked her to B's birthday party while the affair was ongoing. She and the editor had stood next to one another in the garden of Emma's home, holding glasses of champagne, or *rosé* perhaps, while the guests danced in a marquee. I also knew about the yoga teacher, the wife of the country neighbour, the cleaning lady at the holiday home and the number (if not the names) of all the other women B had had sex with, at which I had pretended to be a little bit shocked, a little bit impressed.

In his study, B kept a nineteenth-century mahogany cabinet with many tiny drawers which had once been used in a post office. Each drawer contained a trophy from a woman he had had sex with, often a clipping of pubic hair. This is the kind of thing that serial killers do in movies, and I suspect that B thought he was being cynically ironic with just a dash of danger when he cut the black lace trim off a pair of my knickers in the garden of Montague Square late one night and told me that he would be putting it in 'my' drawer. He had brought a small penknife with him for the purpose.

In his essay on Baudelaire and *Les Fleurs du Mal*, Paul Bourget describes 'the ominous inability to procure for [the] overwrought senses even a single complete throb of pleasure. An indescribable nuance of spleen . . . settles over the libertine who is no longer capable of arousal. His imagination grows febrile, he dreams of pain and of causing pain, to obtain that intimate tremor that would be absolute and total ecstasy.'

Bourget is both precise and discreet, but another way to put it would be that never mind what he had squirrelled away in the mahogany cabinet B could no longer get it up.

*

Elaborate roleplay was required for B to achieve and maintain an erection for long enough to reach orgasm. He outlined the scenario to me after the main course at our first lunch, as though we were having a pitch meeting. We were eating at a Japanese restaurant in a mews off Berkeley Square. Waitresses in kimono clacked between the widely spaced tables in wooden *geta* sandals. In his fantasy, B was a Roman patrician who had sent his 'slave-mistress' to the market to buy a new slave. He specified that the imaginary slave-mistress looked like the popular day-time television presenter and one-time winner of 'Rear of the Year' award, Carol Vorderman. I managed not to laugh.

The slave (me) would be delivered having been duly dressed in a suspender belt, stockings and 'panties'. A leather collar would be fastened around her neck and she would be handcuffed before being 'inspected' to determine if she was fit for purpose. This involved B looking at the slave's teeth, measuring her proportions with a tape measure and shining a small flashlight into her anus and vagina. After this, the slave would be disciplined, to demonstrate her obedience to her 'master' (who was B). B owned a selection of riding crops and folding whips to administer the beatings, which, he warned me, the slave would find 'cruel'. At all times the slave would address B as 'Master'.

I could feel B watching me, waiting for a reaction.

'What happens next?' I asked, with a neutral smile.

'The slave has to beg the master for mercy.'

'Mercy. OK. And then?'

'The slave is rewarded for her good behaviour.'

Bourget observes that the desperate debauchee fantasises about feeling pain as well as causing it. Spending money unnecessarily caused B acute pain, but it also got him off. He said that he would give me a hundred thousand pounds to be his slave for two years.

'You're offering to buy me?'

'Exactly.'

I was silent.

'I've spoken to my accountant,' said B after a while. 'There's a way to do it legally, tax-free.'

'That should be all right then.'

B would visit me at my flat one afternoon a week, during school hours, and I would further engage to have a weekly dinner with him if he had the time. I would also visit him at his home on request and accompany him on trips. B explained proudly that he often travelled to international literary festivals, where he was put up in the best hotels.

At the beginning of our relationship, I was strongly attracted to B. I was certainly intending to have an affair with him, and the prospect of the money made the slave part easier to get along with. I did not point out to him that he was paying me, if not for sex *per se*, then for a particular kind of sex, since as he then and subsequently often pointed out, he did not believe in paying for it.

*

After the lunch, on the way to pick my daughter up from school, I stopped at the hardware shop where I would later purchase the chain for my door that I thought would protect me from Anne Clarke.

That day Mr Ali sold me a large brass hook, the kind used to suspend hanging baskets of flowers outside pubs. I also bought an electric screwdriver which I learned how to use by watching a video on YouTube. Once my daughter was in bed, I attached the hook to the supporting pillar between the kitchen and sitting area of my flat. My mother saw it next time she came to visit and asked what it was doing there. I said it must have been left over from when they knocked the two rooms into one and how funny I'd never noticed it before.

*

Once a week, at five to two in the afternoon, I drew the curtains over the front window. I would already be dressed in the stockings, suspenders and "panties". B would arrive with a small suitcase containing his equipment (now I understood about the convenience of the folding whips), which included a pair of genuine FBI-issue handcuffs. After a bit of time spent with me in the handcuffs looped over the hook I had attached to the pillar, being 'inspected' and then 'disciplined', matters would be brought to a conclusion on the sofa, after which we would have Earl Grey tea with scones and clotted cream. I provided the tea. B brought the scones and cream with him in a separate section of the suitcase, complete with miniature jars of Tiptree raspberry jam. As I came to know his otherwise miserly habits, I suspected that he pinched the miniature jams from the best hotels in which he was accommodated as a guest at important literary festivals, but I appreciated the trouble he had gone to, especially as he had been entirely serious about the 'cruel' part of the proceedings.

I did not feel demeaned or degraded by these activities. As I became accustomed to the script, which never varied, I could anticipate the various stages of pain which would bring B to full arousal. I counted through them in my head as he went about his mastery, as I had once recited French verbs or the reigns of the kings of England.

*

While we were having tea, we talked. B told me all about himself at some length, and, bit by bit, all about Emma. Her daily routine became as familiar to me as my own. B described it to me with a mixture of pride and dismissiveness, both qualifiers deriving from the fact that he was obviously painfully jealous of the fact that she earned more money than he did. B had been hugely successful financially with his books, but he didn't earn half as much as Emma. The pride was meant to some extent to conceal this fact, showing that B was an evolved, modern man who was not resentful or intimidated by the fact that his wife was paid much more than he was, yet it was also genuine in that B had enormous respect for money. None the less, his descriptions also implied that Emma's wealth was derived from her rigid self-discipline (no time for sex) and her lack of creativity (she was not. after all, a Writer).

After a cup of Japanese green tea with a teaspoon of honey at 5 a.m., Emma exercised for forty-five minutes in the home gym at the house in Oxfordshire whilst watching Bloomberg. By 6.30 a.m. she was showered, made-up and dressed, which gave her time for a cup of black coffee with B who was by now awake in order to take the children to school. 'Dressed' was the word — Emma wore only dresses and high-heeled shoes for work; she favoured Michael Kors for the office and Roland Mouret in the evening. Her driver collected her at 6.40 a.m. On the journey into London, she caught up with emails and phone calls to clients in Asia, arriving at her desk in her Mayfair office by 8 a.m. The office hours were admittedly a bit of a blank, as beyond explaining that Emma had begun her career as a financial analyst, B didn't appear to know anything much about what she actually did. Sometimes, I imagined her striding past a long conference table lined with men in suits and pausing at the top to spin on her stiletto and say, 'So, gentlemen,' in a slightly menacing voice. Her office would have a huge window with a view of skyscrapers — in short, I was as ignorant about banking as B was and my imaginings came from movies and soap operas.

Lunch with clients (diet bars at the ready in the loo), office, then back in the car for paperwork on the journey home at 5 p.m. Emma had the use of a company flat near the Shard if she needed to stay overnight in London for a client dinner or a cultural event at one of the prestigious institutions where she sat on the board. B was allowed to stay with her at the flat but not to use it alone. He minded this, as he minded about the driver, although he could easily have taken a pied-à-terre in London had he wished to. He often talked about doing so, but he was too mean. When he wanted to have sex with me in the evening, he would book Claridge's for special occasions, otherwise it was a convenience hotel near the Westfield shopping mall, handy for the motorway.

Emma's schedule was designed to allow her time with her children in the evenings, and after family dinner at 7 p.m., prepared by the housekeeper, heated up and served (though not eaten) by Emma on the table in the dining room, which seated twelve at Christmas and where her husband occasionally fucked me, she would be in bed at 9 p.m. On Fridays, dinner was at 8 p.m. and Emma drank a glass of white wine to relax before bed at 10 p.m. She and B watched television in separate rooms in the evenings. B watched the news and various long-winded crime series, whilst Emma preferred reality shows. One of her favourites was about morbidly obese people in America. The cameras followed their trials and challenges as they had their stomachs stapled, failed on their strict diets and frequently became depressed and suicidal. On Sunday afternoons Emma went through the children's schedules for the week, noting what they would need for school on each day, after which she spent time online ordering groceries, kit for the children's sports and hobbies, presents, items required for maintaining the house and garden and her own clothes, which were delivered for her approval to the office in order to take advantage of Net-a-Porter's same-day

Central London service. Once all the orders were checked off her list, she rang her mother.

B said that once upon a time Emma had enjoyed what he called 'a bit of spanking' but that sort of thing was long over. I saw her point. Emma didn't need B's money, certainly not in exchange for the bruises and welts his cock required these days. Plus, between the gym and her job and the children and generally maintaining B's existence with no distractions or interruptions to his writing routine, why should she summon up the energy? Basically, Emma couldn't be arsed to screw her husband and I couldn't say I blamed her.

Being B's 'slave' for a couple of hours a week was by no means the worst job I had ever done. If the renumeration-to-hours ratio, the short commute and the general deadening of hope in the world were taken into consideration, writing press releases for a pashmina company had been far more difficult. I was interested in why B had taken a chance on my accepting a proposal which many women might have found offensive, though I didn't have to look far for the answer. As far as the Internet was concerned, I was already a prostitute.

8. BELLE DE JOUR

In the small town where I grew up the most significant way you could find out about the world apart from books was magazines. The magazines had white girls on their covers and they told you the same things. You could 'have it all', which meant working in a tall office and wearing expensive 'designer' shoes. In order to have it all, you had to be as beautiful as you could be, as thin as you could be and you had to be good at sex. All the covers featured the word "Sex" — *Hot Stuff!, Sex on Holiday*, *Sexercise Your Way to Fitness!*, *Get Your Best Sex Now!* Then there was the advice — 'Men Tell What Women Do Wrong in Bed', 'How to Blow His Mind' — and the lists: '5 Ways to Drive Him Wild', '7 Sex Tricks Every Successful Woman Knows'. At school breaktimes, we studied *More* magazine's 'Position of the Fortnight' at breaktime in our navy uniform skirts and striped ties. The magazines were all we had, all we knew. Sex, shopping and shoes were your reward for starving yourself and believing in your dreams. If you did not end up with enough of either, it was because you hadn't believed hard enough. Millions of girls like me saw these messages every day, for all the years of our adolescence.

*

Before I had become friends with Sebastian, I had briefly been one of his would-be groupies, though 'stalker' wouldn't be too strong a word. As a teenager, I had never had a crush on a pop singer, never plastered my bedroom walls with posters, so when my first crush arrived after I read the "Gutter Life" column, I got it bad. One night my friend Ellie and I got drunk and went to stand outside the house in Meard Street, calling up at the windows. Ellie tried to sing the chorus of the Kate Bush song 'Wuthering Heights'. I wailed that we were starving vampires in need of his richly-opiated blood. Two women tottering and screeching, clinging to the area railings for support — no one gave us a second glance. Sebastian was not at home. After that, meeting him became a sport. We lurked around Soho, trying to spot him.

Ellie was a member of a club which occupied two dingy rooms above a restaurant near Sebastian's flat. Character was provided by the tobacco blooms on the walls, two old-school Lizzies in tweeds and brogues who drank from opening time to closing at the backroom bar and an ancient, reeking dog named Byron which belonged to the manager. The regulars worked at TV production companies and publishing houses. They tolerated the nasty food and the unspeakable lavatory because the club made them feel that they were part of the louche lost Soho where Francis Bacon had held court at the Colony Room and Maltese razor gangs prowled the alleyways. The editor and writers of *The Sensualist* went carousing there and everyone claimed to know Sebastian, though he never appeared. Ellie and I spent several evenings at the club in pursuit of him, drinking filthy red wine and saying 'darling' a lot. Now and then, Byron would bite one of the old lesbians.

Ellie heard that there was to be an exhibition of Sebastian's paintings at the Grosvenor Galleries. The show was called *Les Fleurs du Mal*. Homing in on our quarry, we set out on the bus from Ellie's flat in

Holborn to see if we could talk ourselves into the private view. This proved to be effortless as the 38 broke down and we had to wait for another one because our heels were too high to contemplate the shortish walk, so by the time we arrived there was no guest list, very few guests and no artist.

Sebastian's paintings received a good deal of critical praise, especially after his death, but seeing them for the first time was disappointing. He'd taken the whole 'flowers of evil' thing literally. A reviewer from *The Times* claimed that the flower pictures were 'an attempt to reinvest art with beauty, urgency and power' and a catalogue pointed out that the canvases brooded 'with menace, reminding viewers that nature's charm masks an ancient, indefatigable force'. Baudelaire asked who would dare to assign to art the sterile function of imitating nature, but Sebastian seemed in no danger of being taken for a realist on the basis of his technique. The 'opulent palette' singled out by the critics looked muddy to me. Sebastian's large, sloppy canvases showing rotting sunflowers in daubs of strident yellow were not nearly as exciting as his writing. We left quickly, feeling foolish.

As I wrote this in the black notebook I could hear Sebastian's voice. *They're crap, aren't they, darling?*

A short time later, Ellie and I were invited to spend a weekend at the house of some friends in Whitstable on the Kentish coast. On the Saturday evening, we all went to dinner at a fish restaurant named Wheeler's and when we walked in there was Sebastian. Ellie elbowed me and hissed in a roaring whisper, 'It's him! Look! Dare you to talk to him.'

Feeling even more foolish, I approached his table. Sebastian stood up with the certainty that only he amongst his party would be approached by a stranger. He was wearing his white suit, which unfolded slowly in front of me as he rose to his full height.

'Excuse me,', I said, 'I'm so sorry, but have you got a light?'

'I don't smoke, darling,' said Sebastian, and sat down again.

Ellie and our friends had their heads on our table, weeping with laughter. I laughed too, impersonating my own tongue-tied star-fuckery. It became the running gag of the weekend, every time someone took out a cigarette they would ask for a light and collapse in hilarity. Meeting Sebastian turned from a joke to a challenge. When I got back to London, I asked my agent to set up a meeting with Gaye Garner, the editor of *The Sensualist*. We met at the club. Gaye was an ambitious, highly shrewd journalist who affected a schoolgirlish manner, wearing full-skirted 1950s dresses and giggling at her own naughty jokes. Over lunch I proposed writing a critical column, addressing the 'dirty bits' in canonical books and pictures. She accepted, adding that unlike *Literary Horizons*, which paid its writers in cases of wine, I would be paid £200 per article.

The first piece I wrote was on how bad English literature was at extra-marital sex. I quoted a poem by the Liverpool Poet Roger McGough, which begins 'Today is not a day for adultery' and ends 'At your age, a fuck's not worth / The chance of catching flu.' I went on to write about Chaucer and Pasternak, Cranach and Ingres, but mostly I was interested in the opportunity of being a writer attached to the magazine, as it would ensure an invitation to the Christmas party at the club.

Sebastian was seated in an armchair positioned at the head of the rickety staircase which led up from the ground-floor restaurant, so this time I saw him from his boots upwards. When our heads came level, he reached into his breast pocket and produced a matchbook from Wheeler's restaurant.

'You're the girl from Whitstable,' he said. 'I've been waiting for you.'

*

I continued writing the column for *The Sensualist* even after it had achieved its purpose. I met my husband and moved away from London, though my friendship with Sebastian continued. We conducted our Tuesday tea parties on the telephone. Unlike most men, Sebastian adored talking on the phone. His old-fashioned ring-dial handset stood next to his bed with its red velvet cover alongside the pistol which Sebastian claimed was always loaded in case he felt like killing himself.

I submitted my column by email using a modem. The tech takeover was still incipient, it was not yet usual to ask for the Wi-Fi code whenever you arrived anywhere. Keeping secrets was much easier pre-broadband. In London, Ellie had also become a contributor to the magazine and had become close friends with its editor. One day she rang me up.

'I have reporters outside my flat. They want to know if you're Belle de Jour.'

'I don't understand.'

'The call girl who writes for *The Sensualist*. Everyone thinks it's you.' Ellie sounded both excited and concerned.

I thought for a moment. Some months previously Gaye Garner

had asked me to write a piece in addition to my usual column on the classic Catherine Deneuve film *Belle de Jour*. I hadn't thought anything particular about it.

'You mean the piece I wrote? Why would anyone be interested in that?'

Ellie sighed. 'No. Don't you ever read the mag?'

'No. You can't buy it here.'

'So there's some woman who started writing a blog about working as a call-girl. Then that turned into a column and now she's got a book deal.'

Ellie mentioned the publishers of the book, who happened to be the same house which had published my (by now) second history book and to whom I was contracted for a third.

'So everyone is trying to guess her identity. There are all sorts of theories and one of them is you.'

'Well, just say it's not me then.'

The world of the Soho pubs and after-hours bars felt a long way away from my new life in Italy. What had been an island of drunkenness and despair buried within the pulsing push of the city had become a parody, a place where middle-aged, middle-class people pretended to be pissed-up losers. The tramps and whores and junkies still hung around, but they were reduced to titillating local colour, lost bundles of humanity that the advertising creatives stepped over on their way into the Groucho Club. The great anecdotal reef of sucked out lies had long since been washed over with media offices and Scandinavian bakeries, its striata of broken talent and shattered, shambling genius drowned more effectively by sizzle reels and smoothies than any number of lifetimes' worth of gin-soured promises. Calling everyone 'darling' didn't make you so very special anymore. Sebastian's genuine self-destructiveness might have made him the authentic Soho article, but everyone else was just pretending.

I told Ellie to take no notice. But Belle de Jour did not go away. The papers continued to speculate about her real identity, putting forth different theories. Several male journalists were considered, as was Gaye Garner herself. All the intrigue made for perfect publicity. Her book was a bestseller and became a television series starring the actress Billie Piper. About a year after Ellie's phone call a long article appeared in the *Sunday Times*. The headline was 'Named: The Belle de Jour of the Net.' It was about me.

*

The one advantage to being called a prostitute on the cover of a national newspaper is that ignominy has very little left to offer you.

*

The *Sunday Times* included lots of details about my personal life in order to match my identity with Belle's. At first this bewildered me, as they were things I was sure the newspaper couldn't possibly have known until I worked out what the editor of *The Sensualist* had done. She had set me up.

The agent who had brokered the lucrative book and TV deals was called Horace Chisholm. He was a crony of the editor; they were often to be seen in conclave at a corner table in the club.

The publicity they had drummed up around Belle depended on her anonymity — if her identity was revealed there would be less interest and potentially less money. So they needed a stooge.

Someone (I doubt it was Gaye Garner) knew more about the early functioning of search engines than I did. I had written the piece on Deneuve at her request, which meant that if you looked up 'Belle de Jour' on the creaky Internet you also got me. Some of the information in the article I recalled telling her myself, but much of it was quite intimate. I asked Ellie if she had been pumped for "proof" over the club's revolting wine. She denied revealing any of the confidential details the journalist had included in the article, yet I couldn't see how else they had come out. I stopped speaking to Ellie.

Some people advised me to sue, but I was too poor and too scared to consider going up against a newspaper owned by Rupert Murdoch. As the Internet bloomed, the first thing you saw if you looked up my name was that article. When I went on Radio 4's *Today* programme to talk about my book on the medieval queens of England, the first question the presenter asked me was about Belle de Jour. Eventually, I paid a lot of money I could ill afford to a solicitor to have the article put behind the paywall, which had just been invented, but it didn't make much difference. By then all anyone wanted me to write about was sex, so I could choose to do that or I could choose not to work. The general feeling, with which I mostly agreed, was that it was all my own fault in the first place for using sex as a way to gain publicity for my writing.

When the *Sunday Times* piece was published, I had just had my first historical documentary commissioned. The subject was Caterina

Sforza, known as 'The Lioness of the Romagna', the independent ruler of a medieval Italian state. I had spent months in archives and libraries researching the story of this strong, fearless woman who had defied the armies of the Borgias to defend her city. Shortly after the article came out, I received a note from the production company saying that they would not be issuing my contract after all, as they had decided to drop the project.

My daughter was a few months old and now that Belle de Jour had lost me the documentary, I was desperate for work. Amongst the many journalism pitches I sent out was an article about a collective of women wine makers in Italy. They had joined together to try to challenge the male-dominated world of viticulture, to show that women growers could produce excellent wines. The editor I spoke to said that she couldn't really find a place for that piece, but could I do her two thousand words on adultery by next Friday? Well, yes, I could. I typed it out immediately whilst breastfeeding my child, which would be a plaintive image had I not also smoked several fags at the same time. The article was almost entirely invented, and it concluded with a tribute to my husband, in which I declared I had found someone whose pain mattered more to me than my unfaithful pleasure. Of all the people who wrote unpleasant comments when the piece came out, none of them appeared to have read that far. It was perhaps the most successful piece of journalism I had ever done, yet I knew it would damage me, and it did.

My marriage began to go wrong around this time. There were many reasons why my husband and I eventually came to separate but being asked if his wife was a prostitute can't have been easy for him.

Four years later, a scientist named Brooke Magnanti revealed that she was Belle de Jour. At a party given by 'our' publishers on the terrace of the Royal Opera House 'Belle's' agent, Horace Chisholm, confessed to me over a drunken cigarette that my theory about the editor of the magazine had been entirely accurate. He was a plump, dapper man who wriggled visibly inside his pale grey summer suit when I cornered him and asked him straight out if he had set me up as Belle. Then he recovered himself and gave me a sheepish smile.

'You've got me there!' he shrugged.

I didn't make a scene. Before he meandered off through the crowd, he actually gave me a wink.

Neither Brooke Magnanti, Horace Chisholm nor the editor of *The Sensualist* ever considered getting in touch with me to make amends.

9. DEPENDING

Money is the grounding trope of all Jane Austen's novels, present in every ballroom scene, every carriage excursion. Romantic love is the heroine's privilege and reward, but she is never obliged to contemplate marriage with a man who is actually poor. Choosing the heart over the head is celebrated, when the heart's desire is never anything less than the second son of a gentleman with a respectable future in the Church. Austen was entirely pragmatic about the straitened options available to women within the ruthless paradigm of the sexual politics of her age; without an independent income an eighteenth-century gentlewoman could be a wife, a governess or a whore.

Demi-mondaines are a subject of fascination in Austen's juvenilia but are almost (but not quite) ironed out of the 'mature' novels. The last of these, *Persuasion*, features a minor character called Mrs Clay. Penelope Clay is an impoverished widow who successfully attaches herself to the proud if impecunious Elliot family. She appears to be scheming to marry Sir Walter, the head of the family, but abruptly changes course and disappears to London, where she is said to be 'in keeping' with Sir Walter's heir, William Elliot. Mrs Clay has taken a monumental gamble. She has actively recused herself from any hope of moving in polite circles, but if she can succeed in persuading William to marry her, the magic ring will erase her transgression.

'She has abilities . . . and it is now a doubtful point whether his cunning, or hers, may finally carry the day; whether, after preventing her from being the wife of Sir Walter, he may not be wheedled and caressed at last into making her the wife of Sir William.'

Mrs Clay has no money and two children to support. If she fails, she can look forward to sinking down the hierarchy of mistresses to a future of streetwalking, syphilis and the poor house. If her wits and her will are strong enough, she can marry a baronet and return in triumph to Society. Unlike Austen's heroines, who however straitened their circumstances never have to do without a roof and servants, Mrs Clay has no one to depend on but herself and she chooses her odds with rather admirable courage.

I liked the phrase 'in keeping' in relation to my arrangement with B. H was also pleased about it because he said he worried about my being single. To him it was in the natural order of things that a woman should be 'taken care of' by a man. Now that Sebastian was gone, H was the only man who really made me laugh and whilst I had not forgotten how I felt, bereft and abandoned in that hotel room in Park Lane, holding it against H wasn't going to make Sebastian any less dead.

*

H relished the stories of B's miserliness. There was the time when he promised me a "special shopping trip" and it turned out to be a voucher for Boots that he'd got on points from his loyalty card. Or the time when he tried to help me economise by giving me a (second-hand) copy of a guide called *Tricks for Thrifters!.* I read out bits of it to H in bed. It had advice on useful things to do with candle ends and how to make pairs of tights last longer by cutting them in half when they laddered and wearing two good halves together, like Princess Michael of Kent. I never wore tights anyway. When he wasn't helping me to count the pennies, which were his after all, B was nagging Emma about her spending. He told me that he hid their drinks trolley when they gave parties in case any of the guests wanted a whisky or a brandy after dinner, which Emma found embarrassing. He tried to persuade her to order the groceries from Sainsbury's rather than Waitrose and once he had poisoned the children by taking a pizza which was past its sell-by date out of the dustbin and making them eat it for dinner when Emma was away for work.

*

When F telephoned to say he was going to divorce Polly, H advised caution. 'Men always promise they're going to get divorced,' he said. 'I should know.'

F said that he had a 'plot', which I thought an unpleasant choice of word. Nonetheless I agreed to meet him in the small French restaurant in Covent Garden where he had first told me about Polly to hear it. F told me that his suffering had been unbearable and that he had even felt suicidal. He couldn't go on unless we were together. He had decided to put his marital home on the market and when it was sold he would tell Polly that he was leaving her.

'But that's monstrous.'

It was one thing to leave Polly for another woman, but to deceive her into selling her home in the belief that they were moving into a new house together was staggeringly appalling. Moreover, was it even legal? If she had signed the papers under false pretenses, any decent lawyer would take F to the cleaners. Surely the only correct thing to do was to tell Polly the truth and work out a suitable settlement — perhaps she could remain in the house, which was also her children's home: that might be better solution for them all?

'No,' said F, 'this is the only way.'

He had announced his 'plot' to me in January, when, according to our agreement, I was to be 'in keeping' with B for the next nine months. It was absolutely clear that B would not leave Emma, but he said that he wished our relationship to continue, a sort of rolling contract. I don't know if B assumed I was sexually faithful to him, or if he took it for granted that I was, or if he simply wasn't interested; whichever way, he never asked.

F wanted to be with me, to make a real family, a real home. We loved each other. If I wanted to be with him, I would have to make myself party to his 'plot' to deceive Polly into selling their house. It was rather late in the day for scruples, but it troubled me that F wasn't prepared to face being open and starting afresh.

F said that if he committed to me, he would expect monogamy, I said that if he committed to me, I was prepared to be monogamous, but I wouldn't expect it from him, which unnerved him. If F had set the house sale as the signal for that commitment, he could have it, but in the meantime I would honour my engagement with B. F had no idea of B's existence in my life and, if he turned out to be lying about divorcing Polly, I thought I might as well be a cliché with some money in the bank. I ran the situation by H and he agreed that this was the prudent course of action.

*

F's house took a long time to sell. He blamed Polly for spending so much of the restoration money on luxury groceries, which meant that the renovations had never been properly finished. F grew increasingly frantic as every few weeks the agents lowered the asking price. Polly supposedly believed that they were moving to the country, which would be better for the children. My private opinion was that she knew something was up. She and F had been married for twenty years. Perhaps he had come close to leaving her before but had proved too cowardly. It didn't inconvenience me if she was waiting him out.

An offer for the sale was finally received in July. This was not ideal, because I was planning to go to the South of France for a whole week with B. The trip had been carefully worked out: B was appearing at a festival in Montpellier and had told Emma he wanted to drive down and spend a few days writing at a quiet hotel. My daughter was due to go on holiday with her father, so I would be free. It seemed precarious. If F found out that I was with B just as he was about to tell Polly about the divorce he wouldn't go through with it, but by now I had conceived a rather peculiar sense of honour where B was concerned. We had an agreement. It was only thanks to B that I could continue paying my rent and the fees for my daughter's school. I owed him. However, F said that he didn't want to say anything to Polly until the state school term was over, in case it upset his children's exams. I said I understood perfectly. Perhaps it would be sensible for us not to be in contact for a few weeks, until this delicate period had passed? He thought this was very understanding of me.

So I went to France prepared to show B a good time. My honourable feeling did not last long. To begin with, B had really upped the ante on the 'slave' front. The hotel where we were staying had been constructed from an entire abandoned *bastide*, high on a cliff above the Mediterranean. The restaurant and other public rooms were at the centre, whilst the bedrooms, which had twee names like 'La Vieille Epicerie', were converted from individual houses scattered along the slopes below. Our room was the former wine press. It stood in a walled garden shaded by a trellis of vines and the grape-treading floor had been converted into a large hot-tub.

In the privacy of the garden, I was supposed to parade around on a chain leash attached to a thick leather dog collar, in nothing but high heels and a black satin corset belt. I suspected B had been at *The Story of O*. The whips had been supplemented by a riding crop with a leather strop and a long, slender white cane that inflicted thin welts which came up deep purple along the backs of my thighs. Worst of all was a metal contraption which resembled a squid with its tentacles folded. B had bought this from one of the medical supply shops round Harley Street. The body of the squid contained a wheel which jacked open the tentacles when it was inserted into the vagina. B's latest variation on 'inspection' involved getting a good look at my cervix.

B was also giving free rein to his penny-pinching tendencies. I was not to drink the mineral water from the mini bar as it was a 'rip off'. Brackish tap water was perfectly good. Taking breakfast on the hotel terrace, beneath a wall of glorious tumbling jasmine, was also a rip off. Every morning, B sent me to the *boulangerie* attached to the petrol station on the main road for croissants or pastries while he prepared coffee with the in-room Nescafé machine. The petrol station sold English newspapers too, and I would bring back *The Times* or the *Daily Mail* for B to read over the dry, industrial-quality pain aux raisins. B would always get very exercised about whatever outrage was in the day's paper. I have noticed that the older men get, the more they seem to need to keep up with the news, as though current affairs are a substitute for their own declining virility, providing an alternative sense of agency or illusion of control. Halfway through breakfast, B would fold his newspaper under his arm and announce that he was retiring for 'a natural break'. I was then expected to wash up the crockery in the bidet and lay it out on a hand-towel to dry with the stench of his crap swirling round the bathroom.

*

In the evenings, B liked me to dress up. When we had first met, B had worn a uniform which he considered rather daring and bohemian — jeans with a heavy, silver buckled belt, dark shirts and a leather jacket. I had persuaded him to try tailored shirts from Turnbull and Asser in Jermyn Street (Sebastian's shirtmaker), with some classic blazers and good leather shoes. Unfortunately, B's new interest in fashion had now extended to my wardrobe. Following Emma's efficient online shopping example, he had set up a secret Net-a-Porter account and had dresses delivered to my flat. I was actually quite impressed that he had found anything so horrible on the site until I realised he was getting them from the cut-price version, the Outnet, where they flog off unsellable pieces. B thought I looked lovely in wrap dresses, very tight, with loud prints, lace trims, sheer panels and plenty of 'fun' styling. Combine in one garment all the most hideous details you can shove on a frock and you get my Riviera eveningwear. B wore the stylish linen suits and summer loafers I had suggested to him while I had to trot along next to him in stiletto sandals and the awful dresses. I winced behind my sunglasses every time we walked into a restaurant and the women turned round to sneer.

B had made reservations at a different Michelin-starred restaurant for every night of our trip, and then complained that the prices were a disgrace. I suggested we try simpler brasseries where the food was good, albeit less elaborate, but B insisted on the starred restaurants. He liked to think of himself as a famous writer enjoying the best places on the Cote d'Azur with his glamorous mistress. However, he could not bring himself to pay for anything other than the house wine and one main course apiece. He made up for this by telling me to stuff the bread into my handbag so he could make himself a late-night sandwich with processed ham from the petrol station. In between the dinner and the ham sandwich, we had to get into the hot tub.

It was still about 30 degrees in the evenings, but B wanted to watch the stars whilst reclining up to his neck in that giant Petri dish of boiling water and former guests' bodily fluids. The chlorine stung the welts on my body and made my skin dry and itchy. Once in the hot tub B would pour us a glass of champagne which came from a case he had bought from duty free on the car ferry. After measuring out the bubbly in our two flutes, he stuck a metal spoon in the bottle, which everyone knows doesn't stop it from going flat. I don't like champagne, but I obligingly raised my glass as B made his nightly toast: 'To a sunny place for shady people.'

I didn't tell B I knew it was a quote, attributed variously to Somerset Maugham or Noël Coward. He was delighted with himself, but between the dresses and the hot tub and the contraption I had stopped prioritising the money, try as I might. I was beginning to loathe him.

On the fifth day, B had a message from his literary agent. He was very excited because Gerard Depardieu had been in touch. Depardieu wanted to buy the rights to one of B's books and turn it into a film. Could B go to Brussels to meet him?

For once I was genuinely impressed (this was before Depardieu had become a crapulous grotesque). 'Wow,' I said. 'Gerard Depardieu . . . *Les Valseuses* is maybe my favourite film.'

B adopted a concerned expression, perhaps to disguise the fact that he had only seen Depardieu in *Green Card*. 'I'm afraid you won't be able to come with me, darling. It might be . . . indiscreet. Will you be able to manage for a night on your own?'

I hadn't hoped for a moment that B would take me with him. I said I'd be terribly lonely without him, but that of course I understood. He couldn't possibly pass up such a boost to his career. Might I be allowed to ask a girlfriend to come to spend the night with me? It wouldn't cost any more. B seemed quite pleased that I would be chaperoned in his absence, so while he made arrangements for the trip to Brussels, I rang up my friend Annabelle.

*

Annabelle had spent most of her life in Paris, but a few years before she had decided to make a fresh start in the south after an unhappy love affair and now lived in Aix-en-Provence. As part of her self-designed recovery programme, she had visited a 'regression-therapist', who took people back into their past lives. Naturally Annabelle had not spent her past life grubbing about in a turnip field before dying of the Black Death as a twenty-five-year-old mother of seven. She was convinced she had been the abbess of a medieval convent, where she had given shelter to Cathar heretics. Annabelle was keen on the Cathars because they had privileged women's spiritual contribution to their movement. In *her* past life she had managed to escape the fate of most Cathar women - being burned alive. Her convent had a garden filled with great clumps of fragrant herbs, sage, rosemary and mallow, and ancient, ligneous apple trees. Annabelle imagined herself walking in this tapestried setting in her linen shift and woollen habit, carrying her exquisitely illuminated *Book of Hours*, whenever she felt lonely or anxious. Now she believed she was a medieval abbess, Annabelle said she felt much better, so you couldn't say the therapy hadn't worked.

She drove over from Aix in her red Mini, arriving a few hours after B left for Nice airport. We swam in the hotel pool and lay on sun loungers, chatting all afternoon, then ate dinner on the lovely jasmine terrace. I ordered foie gras and lobster and two bottles of Château d'Esclans Garrus and charged the lot to B's tab. Instead of sitting in the hot tub I showed the slave kit to Annabelle. She was most impressed with the contraption, perhaps because it had a medieval air. We acted out the whole script, with me playing B, but we laughed so much we had to keep stopping to pee.

I had asked Annabelle to pick up some black bin bags at the

petrol station. In the morning we stuffed them with all the slave gear and threw them into the boot of the Mini. The wrap dresses I left the folded up in the wardrobe of the Wine Press room. We were Thelma and Louise as we drove away. We dumped the bags in a dustbin in the square of the first village we drove through, but Annabelle got lost in a one-way street so we had to circle round through the square again where we spotted a tramp examining the riding whip. He looked a bit disappointed. We were laughing so hard Annabelle couldn't drive, so we stopped in a proper café with a faded blue sign and old men playing *pétanque* under the plane trees for a refresher and a fag. I only just made my flight to London.

*

The sale of F's house dragged on and on, or so he said. It was the end of the summer and still he had not told Polly. He accompanied her to view a cottage near the small Dorset market town of Blandford Forum as though they were still a couple, with not a word about their impending separation. Polly had never liked London and was looking forward to her new life. She was planning the garden and investigating the best ways to keep chickens. 'She has very green fingers,' F told me.

My flat in London had a tiny terrace, just large enough for a small wooden table and chairs and a few tubs in which I failed to grow anything except dreary, unkillable London ivy. We were sitting on the terrace late one evening in September when I asked F where he was planning to live when Polly moved to Dorset alone.

'With you, of course.'

*

My daughter had not shared her home with anyone but me for years. How would F feel if I said I was suddenly moving in with his children, a woman they had never met, the woman who was taking their mother's place in their father's life? I had envisaged a period of readjustment for everyone, particularly because of the children. F might rent somewhere short term in London, for six months or so, and after the announcement had been made and the divorce put in train, adults and children could all meet. Once everything had been given some time I could give up my flat and we could look for somewhere to live together.

That wouldn't be possible, F said. He felt duty-bound to buy a new house for Polly and the children; it was the only correct thing to do and that was that. I knew that the house had fetched a disappointing price, but given that Dorset was so much less expensive than London, surely there would be enough change for a modest, short-term rental? F looked cornered and not just because the terrace was so small. He took one of my cigarettes, puffed at it and choked.

'There are debts,' he eventually began.

F was not selling his house in order to be free to start a new life with me. He and Polly had been living beyond his earnings as a writer for years. They had borrowed and borrowed and borrowed, hundreds of thousands of pounds, from the bank, from friends. Now F was broke. To pay back all the loans which were now being called in, they would have to 'downsize'. So, faced with the option of moving to a small cottage in the country and sharing it with Polly, F had elected to leave her for me. He could carry on living as a writer, typing in cafés and going to literary parties. F was acutely anxious to continue appearing to be successful. He couldn't have people seeing that he had moved to Dorset because he was skint. Abandoning his big house to move in with his lover was romantic, bohemian. Altogether, I was the best of a bad job.

Smoking my own cigarette in silence, I felt a crackling, cackling sensation, a current burning up through the core of my body. Had I really expected that F was giving it all up for love? It wasn't as though I was exactly a model of financial brilliance — without B by now I too should have been in a similar position. Continuing to see him behind F's back had been a practical, reasonable choice. Like me, F had calculated his odds. However disappointing the backstory was in reality, those odds still worked out in my favour. I would still get what I wanted.

We had years and years to work, to get things back on track. If F could sell one screenplay, it might change everything. And how could I blame him for wanting to do the right thing by Polly and the children, to see that they were secure? I told F that it didn't matter a bit, that I loved him come what may and that was the only thing that mattered. We decided that he would tell Polly at the end of the month and move in with me while my daughter had her half-term holiday. I could prepare her for the change in the meantime. It wasn't ideal, but we were both adults, we could accept that things would be imperfect.

H said I was a fool.

10. SOFT FURNISHINGS

In the drawing room of my parents' house, placed opposite the sofa and the glass coffee table, was an antique armchair. The chair was what is described as a "good" piece in that the wooden legs were hand-turned mahogany and the springs were deep and solid, but it was upholstered in an ugly, tightly patterned floral chintz. My mother had spied the chair in a market in the Cotswolds and insisted on buying it, despite my father's protests that we had no way of getting it back home. In the end it was roped to the roof of our car, where it clattered and thumped in rhythm with my father's swearing all the way up the M6. The plan was to get the chair recovered, but it never happened, not because my mother never got round to it — she is a great one for getting round to things — but because there was never the money, or at least, never money that could be spared from something else.

My mother had chosen an olive-green velvet from George Henry Lee's in Liverpool for the chair's renaissance, several metres of which sat for years wrapped in tissue paper on the top of the wardrobe in my parents' bedroom. Whenever she tried to find expert workmen who knew about antique furniture to do the job their estimates were always too high. We endured the chair for years. At least it was comfortable, and when you sat in it you could see from our small, high town all along The Wirral to the Mersey estuary.

My mother said: 'One day, you know, I looked at that armchair and thought, "I don't care if you never get re-upholstered." Somewhere in my subconscious I knew that I wouldn't have to live with it forever, though it was years before I divorced your father.'

*

The precise moment of a decision is never found where we initially imagine it to be located. Cause and effect are safeguards against contingency, the terrifying mutability of our own caprice. We tell ourselves, 'I decided this and therefore this or that outcome was the consequence,' neat as a mathematics problem diligently written up in an exercise book. Yet decisions hide elsewhere, in small connections, plenteously tiny. Actions are the symptom, the dramas which allow us a sense of agency — the dramatic quarrel, the flinging of possessions into the suitcase, the tearful cab ride, but the cause is the laugh that rings too shrill, the tenacious speck of rocket spoiling that otherwise delightful lunch on the piazza in Arezzo, the chance glimpse of the known body which suddenly appears intolerably alien. Here the future is made quite plain, though we do not hear the quick hum of determination.

The joke was funny, the offending leaf was discreetly removed, the body resolves into the beloved contours and on we go, but the moment remains, gentle and insistent, until it can no longer be borne unless we construct from it the narrative of boredom or selfishness or neglect which swells until it fills the room and flight is the only option.

*

When my mother and father separated, he threw the antique armchair in a skip and bought a new one from Marks and Spencer.

Did someone spot the floral chintz and fish it out? Perhaps the chair travelled on to another home to become the focus of another wife's disappointments. Or perhaps it was retrieved by a man whose wife loved bright, fussy patterns, who was delighted with his find and thinks of how lucky she is each time she sits in it. What became of my mother's olive-green velvet is unknown.

*

F and I started hating one another within twenty-four hours.

*

Since we were going to be together, I decided that I should try to appear more relaxed, less "mistress". As a gesture of intimacy, I did not close the door of my bathroom the next time I shaved my legs in the bath. I continued chatting to F as though it were the most natural thing in the world. That this was absolutely inimical to my own notions of privacy, that this was a gift I was attempting to give him, a signal of trust and togetherness, did not appear to enter his head.

He looked affronted, 'I didn't know you shaved your legs.'

I smiled tightly, drawing the razor through the lather on my knee. "What did you think I did?'

'I don't know. I thought you didn't need to.'

No, I thought. I don't shave my legs. Or colour my hair or bleach my teeth or exercise every day or tweeze my nasal hairs or wax my pussy or pumice my feet or exfoliate my skin or dye my eyelashes or use five differently targeted face creams and serums that each cost more than your shoes.

The next morning, I brought F coffee in bed for the first time. One of the first things he had done when he arrived at my flat was to set a small white plastic box of artificial sweetener on the kitchen counter. I clicked two pellets into the cup, added milk, stirred. I hadn't known about the sweetener. It was irrational to be revolted by it, but I was. *If you want to watch your figure, just take your coffee black.* It seemed precious, niminy-piminy, unmanly. Also it was faintly disgusting to drink coffee first thing, before water, before brushing your teeth. After he had drunk his coffee the smell of F's breath reminded me of the thick fug that seeped through the staffroom door when I was at school. This was intolerant of me of course, as maybe the sweetener was F's equivalent of my pink razor, a little revelation of who he was.

F planned to spend the day working in the London Library, but before leaving he had to send off a piece of work. He sat at the kitchen table and fiddled with his laptop. What was the Wi-Fi code? I copied it for him on a scrap of paper from the router. The piece he was sending was stored on a USB stick but he couldn't get it to connect properly. Could he try my computer? I opened it up for him and logged into his email account to get him started. It was impossible for me to begin my own work until he left the table, left the house in fact, so I went upstairs and tidied the bedroom, collected some laundry, pottered tensely about. An hour later F was still sitting in my space, still using my laptop, inundating the whole room with his presence. He knew I had a deadline, yet there he sat, exchanging emails with his editor, entirely relaxed, his long legs sprawled under the table. It was an acute and powerful affront, a denigration of my work and my time compared to his. I would never have done such a thing, or if I had to, because it was urgent, I would have tried to accomplish what was necessary immediately and with many apologies. Yet here I was, hovering by the kettle, meek. Another halfhour passed.

'I'm sorry, but I need my laptop back.'

'OK, I'll just finish this.'

'No, I need it now. I can't work with anyone here.'

I wasn't being aggressive. We were in a relationship, it was important that I should be honest about my needs and feelings. I didn't add that he was treating me like his secretary.

'Oh, darlin'. . . you should have said.'

What I *should have said* was have we not had endless and intense conversations about our work routines in which you nodded along and promised that you would always understand and respect my need for silence?

'There you go.'

He closed the laptop as though he was doing me a favour and collected his things with no particular haste. He went for a pee, looked for his scarf, sent a text. It began to feel deliberate, but finally he was at the door, where we kissed as though we were still in love.

'See you tonight, goddess.'

I held him close. 'Isn't it wonderful? I can't believe it. I'm really going to see you tonight.'

'And the next and the next and the next.'

Everyone knew that everyone was lying.

*

Within days of our cohabitation, I had conceived a potent physical distaste for F. The thick rind of skin on his heels revolted me. I had never noticed before how thin his lips were, and how prone they were to becoming chapped, so that there was always a white flake of mouth-dandruff on his chin. F did not shower before changing his shirt in the evenings, just washed standing up, running a flannel over his armpits and groin at the bathroom sink — a 'whore's bath' in the old-fashioned phrase. This too repelled me. In fact, I considered he did not shower nearly often enough. His teeth began to look yellow and rabbity, with an overlap in the bottom row which ought to have been corrected in childhood.

For his part, F continued to find me disappointing too. 'You look-smaller,' he said one evening as we walked to the cinema at Marble Arch.

I was wearing Converse rather than high heels. 'We've never done much walking before,' I replied.

*

We were invited to the evening reception for the wedding of the son of one of F's colleagues, which was taking place in the courtyard of a converted stables in the East End. F was clearly pleased to have been asked, as the colleague was a highly successful Hollywood screenwriter, so I was keen to make a good impression for his sake. The dress code on the invite was 'Urban Rustic', which gave an idea of the sort of people they were, though F didn't find it funny. I chose a dress which I thought suitable for such an occasion, in flowing striped silk with a long skirt and full sleeves, pretty enough but demure. No female guest at a wedding should ever give the impression she is trying to outshine the bride. The stableyard had been got up with haybales and lanterns set in scrunched-up feed sacks. There were white flowers and greenery everywhere so it looked very pretty, if a bit affected for Hackney. F and I were sitting on a haybale when the father of the groom, the famous screenwriter, came up to say hello. In deference to F's views on flat shoes I was wearing very high leather boots, the heels of which caught in the hem of the dress as I stood to shake hands. I had to do a sort of strangled hop, bobbing like a heron as I congratulated him. Later, there was dancing, for which the bride and her bridesmaids changed into sequinned mini dresses with scooped-out backs. F watched them longingly. I felt clumsy and dowdy and hopelessly middle-aged. In short, I felt like Polly.

*

The problem was that most of our relationship had been conducted drunk. Not staggering-around-legless pissed, but a steady, after hours, three-bottles and why-not-a-brandy affair. I discovered that I couldn't bear to have sex with F sober. F's style of fucking had pleased me before, but now it bored me terribly. It seemed to go on forever because F had learned what he referred to as 'edging', bringing himself to the point of orgasm and then stopping so that he could carry on. I had told him how marvellous this was, that he screwed like he was seventeen, so I couldn't exactly blame him for being put out when I asked if he could hurry up a bit.

'But edging is the foundation of my entire lovemaking technique,' he said.

I had allowed a man who used the phrase 'lovemaking technique' into my bed, my home, my life.

*

During lunch at the Pizza Express opposite the British Library on the Euston Road, I told my friend Cathryn about the embarrassing incident with the famous screenwriter and the trapped hem. She didn't find it funny, probably because it wasn't.

Cathryn had known about my relationship with F for some time. 'Isn't F in Paris?' she asked.

'Paris? No, he's in London, with me. Actually, I suppose I can tell you now. He's moved in.'

'Really? Oh, that's wonderful! I'm so happy for you.'

Cathryn had written several historical biographies of women and was presently working on Mary Queen of Scots, while I was looking at the reports of the Venetian ambassador to the court of Mary Tudor in preparation for a book on Elizabeth I. We sat opposite one another in the Rare Books Room and spent much of our lunchbreak arguing agreeably about our respective subjects. I maintained that Mary Queen of Scots was a fool, an arrogant, spoiled, politically naïve woman who got what was coming to her, whereas Cathryn saw her as a shrewd operator strategising as best she could against treacherous odds.

'I must be mistaken then,' she murmured.

Cathryn was the most lucidly intelligent woman I knew and she was also very kind, the sort of person who never says anything nasty if she can help it. I didn't understand.

'No, tell me, please. It's fine.'

Cathryn pulled out her phone. She was much more assiduous than I was about keeping up with her publisher's demands that she used Instagram. I hadn't looked at F's account since I had snooped on Polly.

'He's posted twice from Paris. Look.' She turned the screen towards me and considerately pretended to be interested in her chicken salad.

F had posted a selfie taken in Place Vendôme and another one at a café table. In the reflection of his sunglasses you could discern a Diet Coke.

'I don't get it. These are old pictures, they must be. He was at my flat this morning.'

'I'm sure there's an explanation.'

'Of course.'

The explanation was that F had not in fact told Polly he wanted a divorce. As it was the school holidays, she had accepted the invitation of a generous friend who had offered her house in South Africa for two weeks and flown to Cape Town with the children. F said he had been intending to tell her about the divorce but hadn't wanted to spoil their holiday.

'So you're posting pictures pretending you're in Paris. Why?'

'I thought it was better.'

'Better for who?'

'The children.'

'Why is it better for them that you are in Paris rather than

London? Rather than on holiday with them? What difference does it make?'

'I told them I couldn't go to South Africa because I had a chance of a screenplay in Paris and I needed to go to meetings. It seemed less suspect.'

'So you're lying to everyone now?'

'I thought you'd understand. I couldn't bear to ruin the trip, they'd been looking forward to it for so long. Polly would have been in pieces, and trying to talk on the phone, with the time difference. . .'

'South Africa is two hours ahead of London. One hour ahead of Paris. Does the time difference really seem like the point to you here?'

This conversation took place in my bedroom, which I had briefly believed was going to be 'our' bedroom. F had been dining at an all-male members' club. He was still wearing his dark navy suit, the same jacket in which I had found the card which told me that his 'arrangement' with Polly was a farce. We had been sitting face to face on the side of the bed. F got up and retreated to the corner of the room, hugging his arms around his elbows. He was shaking, clutching at the jacket's sleeves.

'I love you. You don't know how I'm suffering. For you. For us.'

He was acting, enraptured with his role as the tortured writer. When Cathryn had shown me his fake Instagram posts, I had seen that F had added the words 'Public Figure' to his bio, for the benefit of all 648 of his followers. This was not an exclusive accolade bestowed by the algorithm, anyone could do it, if they were a twat.

F was clever, attractive and the right kind of age. We had many things in common, let alone being 'in the arts', and I was sure that our children would get along. If I could handle this right, it was my chance at reconstructing a family, having a real partner who was also a colleague and a friend. He would recover from the wrench of his divorce, I would support him, we would move on. I had imagined us walking hand in hand in Tangier, up through the sinuous alleys of the Kasbah between the white walls and jewel-painted doorways as cats tumbled through the moth-soft shadows, up through the layered scents of sewage, diesel, cumin, lemon, jasmine until we reached a terrace overlooking the dark breadth of the horizon washed with the clean ozone of the Atlantic.

Which came first, my disgust at F's cowardice and dishonesty, or at his person? Would I have cared about this latest lie if I'd still fancied him? Possibly not. As it was, I had the chance to restore him to his wife with no one any the wiser. He could go back home to Polly before she returned from Cape Town.

'Actually, F, just piss off.'

*

I never saw F again.

11. INTERLUDE

'Maybe you should just try being alone for a while,' several friends told me after the debacle with F. The people who said this were invariably married or living with someone, but they said *alone* as though it was an aspirational hobby, something they'd adore to try if only they had the time, like an all-women surfing retreat in Costa Rica. I brought up a child alone. I paid the bills alone. I'd done birthdays alone and holidays alone and hearing-a-strange-noise-in-the-night-and-creeping-downstairs-wondering-if-you-can-reach-the-breadknife-before-the psycho-strangles-you-alone. What was *alone*, a spiritual fucking Tesco Clubcard? Rack up enough *alone* points and God sends you an email saying click on this link because you've won a perfect boyfriend? At 4 a.m. we all know we're hiring the box from Death, but did they think he was going to be standing there with his scythe in one hand and a lollipop saying, 'You made it alone!' in the other?

*

The contract for my last history book had been fulfilled. With the delivery payment and the remains of B's money for services rendered, I could afford to spend a few months writing another kind of book. There was something I had in mind. Searching through the trunk where I kept my old papers and notebooks, I found a brown envelope with about twenty folded typed sheets inside.

This was the kernel of a novel I had begun many years before, which I had sent to my agent in the days when book manuscripts were still physical objects. It had never got very far and had been posted back to me when the agency moved offices. Most of it was embarrassing to read, but the main character, a young woman who worked in the art world, had a personality which I thought I could revisit. She was clever and educated and ambitious and hardworking, but she was going to learn that because she was poor and had no connections or social safety net the only real power she had was sex. I thought that I would write the sex scenes in the words real people used; the coarse, ugly language that millions and millions of people were tapping into their smartphones with two thumbs every second of every day.

'That woman who writes about sex': I was going to embrace her. Belle de Jour had messed up my life, so if all anyone wanted from me was sex, I was going to give it to them. I would turn the label to my advantage, I would be unapologetic. I would be 'empowered'.

The most famous moment in the life of Caterina Sforza, the subject of that lost documentary, came when the army attacking her besieged fortress dragged her children before its walls and threatened to slit their throats. According to Machiavelli in the *Discourses*, she raised her skirts and showed her genitals, crying out that they could do it, because "here I have the mould to make more". Her children lived. Time had passed and the world had changed. Strong, fearless women were all the rage now, and I was sick of being broke and scared.

So I wrote the novel and it was a bestseller in Europe and for a while my life was very different. No history books, no married men. I refurbished my scruffy flat, I became a VIP Net-a-Porter shopper and I certainly bought a lot of fancy groceries.

Then I started receiving the emails from Anne Clarke and writing about my lovers' wives in the black notebook, which was almost full by now. Anne Clarke had not written to me for some time, long enough for my anxiety at her knowledge of my address to recede. She had frightened me and goaded me, but perhaps she had also helped me. Thanks to her I had looked unflinchingly at those three women — Emma, Lucy and Polly — and accepted the essential unreality of my relationships with their husbands. I had seen what was going on behind the images those men presented to the world and had thought I was well out of it. I had learned that the tenacity of my lovers' wives, their certainty of the truth of their marriages, made me irrelevant, just one more amongst many, one more woman saying 'Yes, but . . .' I had discovered that I wasn't that interested in affirming my version of what had happened. Perhaps I could just disappear from Anne Clarke's thoughts as I realised she had, in the process of my writing about her, disappeared from mine.

The last few pages of the notebook were still blank. How should I conclude?

*

At the end of Emmanuel Carrère's latest novel *Yoga*, the author describes a scene which takes place in a holiday house on Mallorca. He and his female companion have just returned from a walk and the woman starts moving through a sequence of yoga postures. She is young, which he clearly specifies, and the image he leaves with the reader is of her inverted body, performing a handstand. Upside down: '*Sa robe d'été retombe en corolla, découvrant son ventre bronzé* / Her summer dress fell back like the petals of a flower, revealing her tanned stomach.'

Yoga is in many ways a brilliant novel, which examines far more than the technique of Anapanasati breathing — crippling depression, the refugee crisis, the finer points of the execution of Chopin's *Eroica* all feature — but that is where Carrère chooses to finish, with the bare midriff of a fit young woman.

I read *Yoga* as I was considering how to end the story I had written about my lovers' wives. I wondered how it would read if the roles were reversed; if it was an older woman recovering her will to live in the contemplation of the taut, tanned stomach of a young man. '*Ce jour-là*,' writes Carrère, '*je suis pleinement heureux d'être vivant* / On that day, I am wholeheartedly happy to be alive.' Somehow, I doubted that it would have the same effect.

Many novels are concerned with women who lose themselves in love only to lose love and grow stronger in the process. L.S. Hilton was not going to recover her *raison d'être* in the gleam of a new lover's toned abdominals.

But I couldn't close the notebook and put it away in the trunk until I had found the right words.

*

I had shared with Sebastian many of the writers to whom I had been introduced at university by my teacher Professor Nuttall. When he died of a heart attack years later, the obituaries had lauded him as one of the finest scholars and critics of his generation. Together we had read Rochester, Pope and Swift and I attended his lectures on

Shakespeare, upon whom he was considered one of the world's greatest living experts. At a college dinner in my second year, we were seated next to one another and Professor Nuttall told me enthusiastically that he and his wife had just acquired what he called 'a telly box'.

'My wife watches the cricket,' he said, his eyes twinkling in the candlelight, 'and I enjoy the soap operas.'

Professor Nuttall taught me to appreciate Dryden, no longer a fashionable writer, but one whose work, he said, was essential to grasping everything that came after him. On my last day at college, my father and I had hauled my things down the stairs and across the quad to where my mother was waiting in the car. It was cold and foggy, even for June. My feelings about leaving that place were complicated and impassioned, it seemed wrong just to drive away, so I told my parents I was going to take one last walk around the college garden on the roundabout path beneath the Roman walls. Professor Nuttall was also out walking there, I almost bumped into him in the mist. We trod the circuit side by side in silence. When we arrived back at the gate, he raised his soft brown hat and quoted a stanza from Dryden's *The Secular Masque*:

Thy chase had a beast in view;
Thy wars brought nothing about;
Thy lovers were all untrue,
'Tis well an old age is out,
And time to begin anew.

He stood there, holding his hat, as I walked away. Now I wrote out the lines in the black notebook.

It would have been nice, to end it like that.

PART TWO

12. COMMEDIA AL'ITALIANA

An email arrived from my Italian editor. I was pleased to see his name. I had spent much time in Italy for the promotion of the novel and had appreciated his company. He was a delightful man, hugely well read in English as well as Italian, with an idiosyncratic fondness for British sitcoms of the 1970s. He particularly liked *Fawlty Towers*. The email contained four attachments, each one a legal document. A man named Giovanni Piccolo had denounced me for plagiarism and had succeeded in obtaining a hearing against me and my publishers at the Palace of Justice, the main courthouse in Milan.

Several months after my novel had come out in Italy, the publishers had begun to receive a series of letters and phone calls from Giovanni Piccolo, claiming that my book contained themes and passages from *Lisianta*, a novel he had self-published online. Publishers receive such accusations all the time, so they had assumed Giovanni Piccolo was yet another crank and ignored his attempts to contact them. My editor apologised for this, reiterating that these things were very common and usually dissolved if no one paid attention to them. But Giovanni Piccolo did not dissolve. He had hired a lawyer from a well-known Milanese firm, lodged a formal accusation and succeeded in obtaining a writ. The charges were completely absurd, my editor assured me. There was nothing to worry about. However, it was rather inconvenient that the case had progressed so far. 'Italian bureaucracy is incredibly slow,' my editor warned, 'but just because of this you have to act fast and stay ahead.'

As I read and re-read the email, my inbox pinged and pinged. My agent. My British publisher. The head of foreign rights at the British publisher. I ignored them and Googled Giovanni Piccolo. He was easy to find. From his website I learned the following:

He had been born in the same year as me in a small town in Sicily.

His mother was a painter of reputation, who guided him towards his greatest passion, namely Art, by which means he was able to externalise his soul.

As soon as he began to take music lessons, he showed 'authoritative characteristics'.

'He studied ballet and modern dance, discovering the wonderful harmony of the body contained in the balance of the totality of being.'

He had struggled through adversity in the form of his father's untimely death, which unimaginable event had forced a period of deep reflection upon him. After some time, he was sufficiently recovered to devote himself once again to his own pursuits and left Sicily for Rome where he took 'several paths as a commercial agent, reaching professional levels worthy of the commitment he had invested.'

'The profession of representative leads him to move in different Italian cities, which he lives intensely, appreciating the cultural differences found in each of them, and continuing to stimulate his curiosity about Art.'

After ten years, Giovanni Piccolo returned to Sicily, where he published an original study on Leonardo da Vinci, which brought him 'worldwide visibility'.

Last (but only in chronological order), Giovanni Piccolo had published Lisianta. This was the work I was accused of plagiarising.

Giovanni Piccolo was still continuing his research within the paths of Art, in the 'untiring conviction' that implicit in the artist's need to communicate is the request to be understood and loved.

13. ON THE ROAD

When I was promoting the novel, my publishers were prepared to invest a good deal in travel. With the hope of a movie going into production, they had me tour all over the world to push the book in interviews, plus bookshop signings, TV appearances and conferences. On one of these trips, I had spent three days in Mexico City after a twenty-four-hour visit to Buenos Aires. Before South America I had flown from London to Sydney; Sydney to Melbourne; and back to London, inside seventy-two hours. After South America I was to go back to Los Angeles, thence to London to change planes for Rome (where I had met the man with the telephoning girlfriend).

In each of the many cities I visited for the book, I was assigned a guide, or minder, by the publishers of the novel in that country. In Mexico, my guide was a lady named Barbara. She dressed like a war correspondent in khakis, a grey T-shirt and flak jacket with numerous pockets. From the top of her magenta perm to the tips of her Clark's desert boots, she exuded tremendous energy and enthusiasm as she bustled me about. I must see the Metropolitan Cathedral of the Assumption of the Most Blessed Virgin Mary into Heaven! I must try *escamoles*!

I was staying in an enormous hotel built of rose-pink concrete. Wide corridors spread out from a vast, circular central atrium decorated in faux-leather. Everything that wasn't shiny fake leather was carpet, including the walls, and everything was red. Barbara and the driver came to collect me early in the morning. In between a shoot for Mexican *Playboy* (which never appeared), an interview in the home of Mexico's most renowned literary journalist and a TV talk show, I admired the Metropolitan Cathedral of the Assumption of the Most Blessed Virgin Mary into Heaven, and I ate the buttery *escamoles* tacos. The ant larvae were rather greasy and I couldn't say I enjoyed them much. I also got my period.

Mexico City is vast and heavily clogged with traffic, each journey between appointments took at least an hour and our schedule had been itemised to the minute. I had no tampons in my handbag and there could be no question of returning to the hotel, so I asked Barbara if we could stop at a pharmacy and explained what I needed. Barbara looked irritated, 'This will be very difficult.'

We pulled over at several pharmacies, all of which were closed. For the next appointment, with a renowned Mexican journalist, I excused myself and headed for the bathroom, where I wadded a roll of lavatory paper inside my knickers. Barbara looked disapproving. Naturally the renowned journalist offered me a white leather chair. After the interview, Barbara disappeared into a small shopping mall, returning with a box which she thrust furtively into my hand. There was no time in the schedule for me to find a bathroom, so I had to insert the tampon in the back seat of the car. I stuffed the bloody wad of paper into my handbag and wrestled with the tampon, which was the kind with no applicator: you have to position your finger in the middle of the butterfly of cotton wool to get a purchase on it, which is not so easy in a moving vehicle. For the rest of the day, the tampon, which was enormous, hung out of me like a single udder, chafing and leaking.

The last meeting on the schedule was a radio interview to be broadcast at midnight. I don't speak more than a few words of grammatical Spanish, but I can understand what is being said, so had elected to use one-rather than two-way translation in order that precious time would not be lost on the live show. The presenter asked her questions in Spanish, I replied in English via the interpreter. It took a lot of concentration. Eventually the interview finished, the presenter thanked me elaborately, I attempted an equally courteous reply and Barbara and I were back on the road. By now there was blood all over the crotch of my trousers and, I fretted, the car seat. At the rose-pink hotel I trailed up to the red atrium. I knew the number of my room, but the corridors were so long, so identical, that I took the wrong one, and walked around for about twenty minutes. By the time I opened the correct door I was crying with frustration and fatigue.

I yanked out the faulty tampon, showered and called room service . '*Una copa para vino tinto, por favor* . . . a glass for red wine please.'

The order took such a long time to arrive that I was asleep when someone knocked at the door. There stood a young man in a red shirt with a tray. His name badge, inevitably, read 'Juan'. On the tray was an empty wine glass, which he proffered with a pleasant, professional smile. He had brought me just what I had asked for.

I screamed. I lost it. I shouted at Juan, 'Why? Why is it so fucking difficult to bring a glass of fucking red wine?' Then I recovered and began apologising incoherently for my appalling behaviour. I grabbed all the money in my bag, paper notes of all denominations, and thrust them into his hand. '*Lo siento, lo siento!*' I repeated. Juan retreated with another professional smile. I lay on the floor and sobbed into the red carpet until it was soaked.

That was what Giovanni Piccolo was trying to take away from

me. Not potential opportunities to further insult random waiters, but all the work, all the effort, all the exhaustion. The novel had been easy to write, but very difficult to publish. What had been even more difficult was the work of promoting it, of being the person that the publishers and the journalists seemed to have wanted me to be for almost two years. That was what had reduced me to that pathetic figure weeping on the floor of a luxury hotel, whingeing with self-pity. I had done everything that had been asked of me. I had taken the planes and posed for the photographs. I had smiled and smiled and smiled. I had told myself over and over to be grateful, grateful for the first class flights and the drivers, the extravagant launch parties, the bouquets of flowers. This was luck. This was success.

All the time, aside from the overwhelming weariness, I was acutely distressed by all the attention that had coalesced around me. I shivered and shook. I threw up before addressing the literary festival in the Massenzio Basilica in Rome. I retched from anxiety at the conference themed 'Voices of the Future' in Stockholm. I quaked in fear in the French TV studio. I was sick with angst as I shared a sofa on *This Morning* with British national treasures Holly and Phil. I could have said no, of course I could have said no, but I forced myself to do it because *if* the book sold, *if* they made the movie, then my daughter and I would be secure. I felt I had no choice.

*

During the promotional tour in the UK, I was interviewed for the *Daily Mail* by the journalist Jan Muir. The meeting took place in a hotel suite, where I was also being photographed for the piece.

Such interviews usually begin with a few minutes of small talk – where in the city one has travelled from, the weather and all that. Tea or coffee or water is offered. We were sitting at a large table; the photographer and his assistant were setting up lights around the room. Jan Muir accepted tea, which I poured out for her. Then she asked me how many men I had slept with.

The correct response would have been, 'I'll tell you if you'll tell me.'

The honest response would have been, 'I have no idea.'

My response was, 'More than ten.' I felt a fool.

*

I had spent months and months away from my daughter, yet I told myself it was worthwhile. It had to be worth it. It was a job, it was work, and I had to do it with all the energy and grace of which I was capable. I had to act a version of myself in Amsterdam and Munich and Delhi and Helsinki and Madrid, in Milan and Mumbai and Montpellier, in print, online, on TV, because if I failed to acknowledge this opportunity, this extraordinary good fortune, then I would have let myself and my daughter down irredeemably. That was what I believed at the time. I was being the gallant, plucky single mother giving her all to secure her child's future, and however shallow and disingenuous that sounds it was the truth because it had to be. Otherwise, I would have vomited all over Holly and Phil. That was what Giovanni Piccolo wanted to steal.

*

Giovanni Piccolo's website featured a full-portrait photo. He was pale and plump with thick black hair and eyelashes so dark he might have been wearing kohl. A dainty frill of tummy hung over his hips; and he held his hands either side as though arranging a tutu. He was the type to have odiously small feet. I stared at the picture for some time; at this man who had forced his way into my life through the Internet.

My novel had sold very well by Italian standards and there had been a lot of publicity. I had been on the cover of several magazines and done a big shoot for Italian *Vanity Fair*. Everyone had asked when the movie of the book was coming out, and it was implied that I had been paid a great deal of money, which was presumably what Giovanni Piccolo wanted a piece of, as well as the glorious glare of publicity. Did he think that I would be frightened for my reputation and settle for a fat out-of-court payoff? Or could he genuinely believe that I had plagiarised his book?

I opened the PDFs which set out the legal case to date. The declaration submitted by Giovanni Piccolo had been rubber-stamped on 4 November. Then there was a document in which his lawyer formally accepted the case. The remaining two documents outlining the charges which alleged that I had violated Giovanni Piccolo's copyright were divided into two sections, covering the *forma esterna* and *forma interna* of the novel, in other words, its external form – narrative, locations, plot and so on – and its internal form, more specific similarities of language or imagery. The lists were as long as they were ridiculous. My protagonist had taken a phone call on a bench, so had Giovanni Piccolo's. My protagonist had eaten linguine with pesto and green beans, Giovanni Piccolo's had also eaten linguine with pesto, though he didn't mention anything about green beans. There were pages and pages of supposed similarities, all of an equally superficial and spurious nature. Giovanni Piccolo's lawyer might have been able to insinuate that in *War and Peace* Tolstoy had stolen a whole ton of scenes from *Madame Bovary*, but he clearly knew nothing about the publishing industry.

The masterstroke of the lawyer's evidence was revealed with a flourish in the time line. *Lisianta* had been published online a year before my novel was released. In that period, two copies had been sold in the UK. I had therefore supposedly seen the book, copied it, sold it and had it appear in translation in that period. The intense hatred I had been feeling towards Giovanni Piccolo was now muted with contempt for his ignorance. I had sold my novel to the British publishers five months before *Lisianta* had appeared online, and it had then been sold to the Italian publishers at the London Book Fair one month prior to *Lisianta*'s appearance. Were Piccolo and his lawyer seriously proposing that within that month I had obtained a copy, translated it from the Italian, inserted aspects of Piccolo's work and then replaced them in a manuscript which had already been sold? Details of the London Book Fair sales had also appeared in the trade magazine *The Bookseller* and *The Hollywood Reporter*, again a month before *Lisianta* was issued.

It was chronologically impossible. Moreover, I had a copy of the book's first chapter in the original post-marked envelope in which I had enclosed it to my agent thirteen years previously. And since it had taken me several years to find a publisher, I could list at least ten other senior publishing professionals who could testify to seeing my work at least three years before the appearance of Piccolo's, if only for the purpose of rejecting it. The man was no more than an opportunist. No judge could logically countenance the remotest possibility of plagiarism.

I had felt as though I had been physically attacked, but now the adrenalin began to ebb. I lit a cigarette and got to work, going back through my correspondence to track the progress of my book. I called everyone who had seen it and asked for statements, I spoke to my publisher and my agent and by the end of the day we had assembled a comprehensive refutation of Piccolo's allegations, which was collated into a single file and sent to Milan where it was copied immediately to the court. At about 6 p.m., my Italian publisher called to say that in his opinion it was extremely unlikely that Piccolo and his lawyer would proceed with the case.

He was wrong.

*

That autumn night was the last I was able to sleep for some time. Late the next morning, I received another email from Italy. Piccolo intended to go through with the hearing. Everyone assured me it was a mere formality. The case would surely be thrown out, so I was not to worry. I asked to speak to the lawyer representing the Italian publishers, and by extension, me. I was told this was unnecessary, but I demanded to speak to him. I was furious and brittle and shrill. I insisted on knowing which documents would be presented to the court. Were they going to list the supposed similarities between the two texts in a public hearing? Probably, they told me, but why was

I so concerned?

All the people with whom I was dealing professionally were roughly one generation above my own. I could clearly remember a pre-digital world, whereas they by and large still lived in one. They simply had no idea. It didn't matter that the charges were specious, that they were demonstrably absurd. What mattered was that if one bored journalist covering the civil cases beat in Milan put something on Twitter, the charges would become, in some sense, true. They would follow me forever, they would swarm and spread, and I would never, ever be free of them. I would be besmirched. My agent suggested gently that my reaction was disproportionate. I tried to explain that truth had adjusted its boundaries, that what was real was what people read on their phones, that facts were no longer invulnerable. Giovanni Piccolo didn't need to win his case to ruin me, he just needed to state it.

No one said it aloud, but the word *hysterical* hovered in the air.

*

The nerve worm writhed in my guts. It relished my humiliation; its appetite grew as it munched and chattered. Sometimes it lay coiled beneath my ribcage, sometimes it unfurled, swelling to a cackling creature whose snorting and screeching were impossible to still.

I made my daughter breakfast, read to her while she ate it, packed her lunchbox, took her to school and then I spent the day plotting against Giovanni Piccolo. There was no time for writing in the black notebook about Emma, Polly and Lucy.

According to the legal documents, the two copies of *Lisianta* which had been purchased in the UK and upon which Piccolo's case substantially rested had been sold in July and August respectively, that is, several months after the London Book Fair, long after the reading and sale of my manuscript as described in the submission for the defense. I presented this nugget of new evidence to my agent and the British publishers and the Italian publishers who agreed politely that it ought to be passed on.

Most people active on social media are in a state of naïve bliss about the way in which they make themselves vulnerable as they chase after audience engagement. I set up a fake Instagram account to spy on Giovanni Piccolo, my latest crush. He was a keen user and had recently informed his fifty-four followers that 'something big' was coming up soon in Milan. He went so far as to tell them to 'watch out' for an announcement on the day of the hearing.

When I saw that, I tried to insist that I attend, but once again was told it was unnecessary. A week later, Giovanni Piccolo was on the move. In between cigarettes, I refreshed my Instagram feed over and over again. Messina, Naples, Rome, Giovanni Piccolo crawled his way up the Italian peninsula. He seemed excited to have left Sicily, posing for a selfie every few hours. He usually snapped himself giving the victory sign, often in close up, so that however I magnified and span the selfies it was often difficult to work out where they had been taken. I liked them all.

*

The previous summer, I had been invited by the Italian editor I liked so much to a dinner at the restaurant on the top of the Triennale art gallery in Milan. My English editor was with me; we were flying on to Stockholm the next morning. Milan is often muffled in fog or smog or both, but in the view from the terrace which, that night, was extraordinarily clear, it was possible to discern the original outlines of the city which was once considered the most beautiful in Italy. You could see the shape of the early medieval walls, the boulevards running out from the squat mass of the Castello Sforzesco, the avenues which had formerly been canals and in the distance the steep flank of the Alps. This was the place where I had lived with my husband, where my daughter had spent the first three years of her life. I could see the treetops of the Public Gardens where I had taken her in the afternoons and the triumphal arch of Porta Venezia at the top of the street in which our flat had been.

A lady leaned forward and met my gaze across the table, 'You should change places with me, so you can see Citylife.'

Citylife is the name of the new district of high-rise buildings on the edge of town thrown up by Silvio Berlusconi and his cronies twenty odd years ago.

I duly swapped seats and took in the tower blocks.

'*E bellissimo*,' said the lady. 'Milan looks like New York.'

'*Bellissimo*,' I agreed. One of my favourite writers, Sybille Bedford, referred to New York as 'the galvanised grave'. I have always loathed the place.

*

Giovanni Piccolo took a selfie with Citylife in the background. '*Bellissimo!*' he captioned it, '*Sembre New York!*' *He* was in Milan, all ready for his hearing.

He had displaced Anne Clarke, but not for long. I called Pete the Gangster and asked if he was free for a drink.

14. RETALIATION

Pete and I had first met when I lived in East London, long before I married and had my daughter. His nickname was for real as he actually was a gangster. He had served for ten years in the British Army before returning to what he described as the family trade. I had read about Italian mobsters consciously modelling themselves on characters from *The Godfather*, a theme which was taken up in the TV series *The Sopranos*, but if Pete sometimes sounded like a Cockney version from a Guy Ritchie film, it wasn't because he had heard of Guy Ritchie.

We met at the gym – not a spit 'n' sawdust boxing gym but a nice one, with a pool and saunas and a juice bar. After we had crossed over between the running machines and the free weights for several weeks at around 7 a.m., we started to say hello and then found ourselves next to one another in the queue at the Costa Coffee next door. After that we often met up.

It was a mildly flirtatious relationship, in which we quickly slipped into role, his street to my wide-eyed Lady Writer. I think he was as aware as I that this was an exaggeration, a game, and once he felt he could trust me (not that he could, particularly), he enjoyed shocking me. He liked telling stories about celebrities and their connections with London's underworld, some of which may have been true. What Pete mostly did was move stolen goods, driving them around in a van with his brother. The van contained a collection of building tools on a tarpaulin, with the stolen things underneath, which seemed a rather old-fashioned arrangement. Once, on my birthday, Pete took me to the van, which was parked in the Barbican multi-storey car park and said I could choose something. He shuffled back the tarp to reveal flat orange boxes of silk Hermes scarves, real ones, not knock-offs. The one I chose as a birthday gift was a steel blue with a pattern of a panther in peach colour. Years later I wore it on TV and Pete sent me a text: 'Nice scarf! x'

*

I liked being around Pete, even just at Costa Coffee, because he was male in a way that none of the other men I knew were. He didn't swagger, he was never rude or aggressive, but there was something about him that I noticed other men noticing. They kept their distance. I had never seen Pete behave in anything like a violent manner, but quite a few of his celebrity stories ended with a rhetorical question.

'What happened then?' I would prompt him.

'Well, we sorted him out, didn't we?'

Once we were in a pub together (not Pete's local, he lived in Essex, but he liked to start his day of driving stolen goods around London with a workout) when a man came through the door and passed our table, where I had just put down our drinks – white wine for me, a pint for Pete. Pete stood up and blocked the man's way. He said, 'I don't think so, mate.' The man turned round and left without a word. He looked perfectly ordinary, but I didn't like to ask Pete why he had objected to the man's presence and he didn't explain.

After I moved away, we kept in touch, texts at Christmas or on birthdays, and when I returned to London and the novel had come out I often called him and asked him to lunch. Several months before I received the news about Giovanni Piccolo, we had eaten at a Turkish restaurant in Hackney where I asked Pete lots of questions about the army. One of the failed ideas for the thrillers that my agent wanted me to write involved an army widow, but it never came to anything.

*

London was already lit up for Christmas, necklaces of lights streaming down through the city towards the greedy clutch of the West End. Soho was in full charivari; it was early so the crowds of office-partygoers were still amiable and boisterous, staggering good-naturedly out of the way as the cab slowed to walking pace. From the corner of my eye, I saw a group of girls in miniskirts, heels clacking expectantly on the pavement, arms linked, all lovely and arrogant and out on the lash.

Pete had suggested we meet at the terrace bar of a sushi restaurant in a high-rise building in the City. He was clearly shocked by my appearance, though he disguised it quickly. My face felt all spiky bones and I stank of fags. The skin under my eyes looked like Weetabix.

'You all right, darlin'?'

'No.'

When he came back with our drinks I asked if he knew how to get someone hurt.

'This for one of your books?'

'No. For real.'

I explained briefly what had happened. Pete then asked if I

wanted Giovanni Piccolo "sorted out", which made me smile for the first time in a while.

'How much?'

'Ten grand would do it.'

'And if I didn't want to "sort him out" completely? Just hurt him?'

What I wanted was for Giovanni Piccolo to watch his own leg being broken: that stupid fat little dancing leg. I wanted him to watch in disbelief as his kneecap was snapped backwards, for the surprise to register before the pain; lots of it. I fantasised about him howling in a Sicilian alleyway with shards of white bone splintering from the back of his thigh.

'That? Oh, about a grand. Plus expenses. Flights and so on.'

I told Pete the Gangster I'd think about it.

*

Why don't you stick to writing your own sleazy books, L? Anne Clarke had written another email.

Your books. Your *own* sleazy books. The phrase 'her blood ran cold' is a cliché for a reason, as is 'feeling your veins turning to ice' and cannot be respectably used by a professional writer. Yet that is exactly, precisely, how it felt when I read that email. Beneath my shirt and jumper and coat I was freezing, while hot sweat suddenly ran down my back. Giovanni Piccolo might know nothing about publishing, but Anne Clarke did. Whether she was Emma or Polly or Lucy, she was married to a writer. She knew about lead times and translation rights sales, about the time lag between signature and delivery. Anne Clarke *knew*.

I was in a cab, criss-crossing back across London to catch the babysitter. A quick glance at my phone and there they were: more words like venomous darts aimed at me. Maybe not just me. This attack was different, no mention of her husband or her pain. We were minutes away from my flat. As I leaned forward to tap the glass and tell the driver that I was in the most terrible hurry to get home and could he possibly speed up, I texted the babysitter: I'll let myself in. Please don't open the door if anyone knocks. Nothing to worry about.

The text was delivered, but she didn't respond, so I rang her as the cab stopped behind a truck parked on the corner of my street. Men in high-viz jackets were unloading tables and benches for the Christmas Fair at the Swedish Church.

'I'll get out here, it's fine.'

'They'll be off in a minute, love. No trouble.'

The babysitter answered as the cabbie lurched round the truck and I scrambled to get out of the cab, saying, 'Don't open the front door!'

'What's wrong?'

The babysitter's bewildered voice chirped from my pocket as I fumbled for the fare, fumbled for my keys, crying and wishing the driver Happy Christmas, and nearly banged into one of the porters staggering down the ramp of the truck backwards, dragging a huge painted wooden horse. I clattered into the house and ran up the stairs to find my daughter safely asleep in bed.

*

When I was still writing history books and having affairs with married men, I was good at what used to be called compartmentalisation, defined as 'the ability of an individual to create separate compartments in their life into which uncomfortable internal realities can be placed and thus ignored'. It was one of those words which had made its way from therapists and clinics onto the pages of the broadsheets and the women's magazines, rubbed to a wraith on everyone's tongue. Dysfunctional, codependent, ideation, journey, neural pathway, process, emotional bandwidth, all similarly had their moments. 'Narcissist' has proved enduringly popular. These words, which encapsulate complex psychological conditions and have been used to treat millions of people, have become fashionably reflexive, used without much consideration as to their true meaning. Men were supposed to be better at compartmentalising and readers were warned that it was a sign of emotional damage.

Sitting at the table with the bewildered babysitter paid, still in my coat, I thought that compartmentalising had worked just fine. Closing things off in neat mental boxes, keeping them separate, seemed an entirely rational manner in which to approach the world. Somehow I appeared to have lost the knack. From the time Anne Clarke's first email had appeared, I had been transformed into a panicked, wild-eyed, trembling Olympic-class vomiter, invaded by a poltergeist which wrote my true self on my body in a manner that I couldn't say I cared for.

Anne Clarke hated me the same way I hated Giovanni Piccolo.

I had done to her what he had done to me.

*

What if Anne Clarke was B's wife, Emma? Whether or not Emma knew about the mahogany postal cabinet in B's study she can't fail to have noticed that her husband changed in the months after we met. He lost ten kilos, bought a complete new wardrobe and an Aston Martin, and had a hair transplant, none of which gestures could be described as subtle. But Emma was compartmentalising. Her marriage was fine, her life was fine. And then — imagining Anne Clarke was Emma — I had slipped into her life the way Giovanni Piccolo had slipped into mine. Out of nowhere, I had attacked something that was hers, something she had created — for what are marriages if not stories? — threatening destruction. I was outside the boxes, I was an invader, I could not be tidied away. She had looked me up online as I had done with Giovanni Piccolo. Perhaps she had spent hours staring at me, as I had at him, worrying at the wound, peeling and picking and poking. Perhaps she had lain awake at night, as I had, imagining extravagant scenarios of denunciation and revenge. Had Emma gone through her busy, precisely structured days with the white noise of her loathing thrumming in her ears, her hatred for me the tilt and whistle of an ever-present wind?

*

After hanging up my coat and changing into pyjamas, a sweater and thick socks, I wrote up the latest entry in the black notebook.

I had left several pages blank around the email section, having rightly anticipated that there would be more. The postcard from the National Gallery was paper-clipped to the cover.

Why don't you stick to writing your own sleazy books, L? I copied it down then read all the emails again.

Anne Clarke knew about the plagiarism accusation; she was taunting me with it. There was something else. Flipping through the pages, I found the sentence I had scribbled on Anne Clarke's possible alias, the connection with the du Maurier novel *Mary Anne*. I hadn't looked at my essay on the novel for years but now I stood on a chair to reach the top shelf where my own books were lined up. Still on the chair, I turned to the piece. I had remembered correctly. In describing her character's experiences in court, the essay noted that Daphne du Maurier had drawn on her own experience of standing trial for plagiarism in 1947. She had been charged with stealing forty-six episodes in her bestselling novel *Rebecca*. The accusation was farcical and the case was ultimately thrown out, but du Maurier recalled being forced to discuss her work in such a manner in public as being deeply "degrading". I read my own comment on this: "Du Maurier's image of Mary Anne on the witness stand, pathetic and vulnerable yet self-consciously culpable, highlights the way in which the law can make victims of women whilst being too unsophisticated to determine questions of personal morality."

My ankles gave out as though I was balancing on a paddle board. I had to jump off the chair before I fell. How could it be so? How could Anne Clarke have learned about Giovanni Piccolo? Had there been gossip at my publisher's office? Had an assistant overheard a conversation or read an email, then spoken to someone else, who then told a colleague? — no that seemed too unlikely. H, B and F were practiced adulterers. They would never fall into the amateur's trap of mentioning a mistress's name to their wives. And why would anyone else do so? I wasn't interesting enough for anyone to care. Anne Clarke was purposeful, deliberate.

If I wanted to hurt me, what would I do?

Anne Clarke's second email had referred to her children, and the postcard to my daughter. Children seemed to be relevant to her. When it came to motherhood, H, F and B were unanimous: Lucy, Polly and Emma were all excellent mothers. Between them they had eight children, and their husbands regularly gave me progress reports. I knew who was struggling with Maths GCSE, who had a friend with a worrying habit of self-harming, who was presently vegetarian, who had been chosen for which sports team. Asking after the children of my lovers didn't feel jarring; I was curious to learn about their progress and the different ways in which their mothers dealt with problems. Occasionally, with my own daughter, I would find myself thinking, what would Emma do? How would Lucy have handled this? For a time, I even believed that F's children might become my stepchildren and had imagined having a wise, supportive conversation in which I emphasised that I knew I could never ever be anything like their mother to them, but that I hoped we would be able to become close in time.

*

Emma was the strictest and most authoritarian of the three women. She endured her punishing timetable in order to maximise her time with her children and brought them up to follow her example. Their out-of-school activities were precisely organised and Emma expected them to be punctual and participate fully. She was not draconian, but rather more conscientious and highly engaged; never pushy. Lucy had adored becoming a mother. Unlike Emma who had found her babies draining and tedious when they were tiny, Lucy was the type of woman who finds toddlers charming and loved staying at home with them. She had wanted a fourth child but had developed fibroids which led to her hysterectomy. It had been difficult for her when the children started school, but she had become involved with all sorts of PTA activities, remaining closely involved in their daily lives. Polly was the most indulgent. She was relaxed about homework and bedtimes but according to F she could be fierce in her children's defence. She liked baking with them, and watching old films, tumbled up together under a blanket on the sofa. I admired Emma's thoroughness, Lucy's devotion and Polly's gift for contentment in her children's company.

To my mind the worst thing, the very worst thing you can do to a mother, is hurt their child. Equally, that's why most mothers would be unable to countenance it. Anne Clarke had certainly succeeded in scaring me, as my ridiculous scene with the babysitter had proved, but assuming she was either Emma or Polly or Lucy and therefore not actually deranged, she might imply a threat but would be unlikely to carry it out. She might perceive me as a threat to her children, but she wouldn't retaliate by hurting mine. What then?

*

If I were planning to damage L.S. Hilton I would attack her career, not because she was famous or successful enough for anyone to care about her being publicly shamed, but because if I was Anne Clarke, married to a writer, I would know two things. First, that a plagiarism scandal, or the hint or suspicion or association of a plagiarism scandal, would send most publishers running for the hills. The best you could hope for after that would be work teaching creative writing. Secondly, a book you have made and put out into the world, however feeble or inadequate it may be, is an intimate part of yourself. Even if it's a hack job, written for money with one eye on the clock and the other on the word count, somewhere inside it will be a little piece of your marrow. It would hurt.

*

Anne Clarke's first email had arrived after the novel had been published, her second coincided with the sequel. All along, Anne Clarke had had a plan.

*

How could I determine that Anne Clarke was the reason Giovanni Piccolo had slithered up to Milan? The obvious thing to do was to ring him up and ask him, straight out. His number was on his website and it wasn't the first time I'd thought of using it. Yet since I was officially his legal antagonist, calling him could be construed as an attempt to intimidate him, which would look bad for all the obvious reasons, and not least because I had just returned from having an apparently calm and rational conversation with a hit man.

It was one in the afternoon in San Francisco. I rang up my tech journalist friend, Bee.

15. *SINE QUA NON*

Bee and I had met in London during the last year of the dotcom boom, so our friendship bridged two entirely different worlds. Her articles and interviews about new technologies, start-ups and digital gadgets seemed arcane, but meant she often benefited from promotional offers. Before we had got to know one another well, Bee had suggested that we go to Copenhagen for the weekend as she had found some whizzy voucher on what people didn't yet call online for a weekend at an old-fashioned grand hotel, the Angleterre.

I arrived at the hotel first, to find the lobby filled with huge, banked vases of tulips in every colour from palest parchment to juicy purple. Their mismatched, effortless opulence seemed very sophisticated. I poked my head between the flowers to tell the desk clerk that I was the guest of Elisabetta Stefanelli. The girl took a few moments to find the reservation and when she did her eyes stretched wide.

'*The* Elisabetta Stefanelli?'

'Er, yes. My friend.'

'Oh dear, I am very sorry, madam. There has been a mistake with your room.'

I thought that the whizzy voucher had not been quite so effective and wondered how we would afford to stay in a place with so many tulips casually flopping around.

'Please, if you would like to wait at the bar? A glass of champagne, perhaps? I'll be just a few minutes.'

Bee appeared in the lobby, her Liza Minelli bob gleaming like an exotic mushroom in a wheatfield, wearing her usual navy duffel coat and a huge pair of vintage bug-eye sunglasses. The desk clerk shrieked and flapped her hands, 'Miss Stefanelli! Miss Stefanelli, please come this way. Your suite will be ready in just a few moments, please accept our apologies.'

We never did work out who the desk clerk had mistaken Bee for, but the famous Miss Stefanelli and her friend had a beano of a weekend. Bee kept her sunglasses on at all times and I found myself walking a few paces behind her, a respectful lady-in-waiting. Our bathroom had two tubs side by side in which we wallowed in geyser-hot water with bubbles up to our noses. We went ice skating on Kongens Nyrtov, where our skates were laced up by the handsomest man we had ever seen and drank mulled wine. We were given the best table at the Søren K — an unbookable restaurant named after Kierkegaard: not such an odd choice of name as existential angst and *gourmandisme* often go together — and were driven in a huge pompous limousine to a nightclub where everything was silver and white. Bee taught the Crown Prince of Denmark to dance the corkscrew twist.

*

Bee moved to a loft in Via Paolo Sarpi in Milan with her Italian husband a few years later. The area was the nearest Milan had to a Chinatown and was just beginning to turn towards hipsterism. With my husband and baby daughter, I followed her, settling in a bourgeois apartment where I spent much time in the evenings smoking and drinking wine on the service balcony. Bee and her husband went off to a weekend tech conference and in their absence their landlady turned the loft into a love hotel for her Ragdoll cat.

The landlady wanted the cat to have kittens and had procured a potential father. To give the cats private time together she covered most of Bee's furniture with old sheets and let them at it. Bee returned to find her flat stinking of tom spray and catshit and her kitchen cupboard full of organic quinoa and blueberry catfood, but the Ragdoll cat had failed to conceive. When Bee was next planning to go abroad, she noticed an advertisement for a Ragdoll tom taped to the lampposts in her neighbourhood. She feared her flat would again be the rendezvous for a breeding date, so I called the number and told the landlady I had a suitable cat. She was delighted. Where should I bring the cat, I asked? This time, the landlady gave another address, so I said I'd call her back.

I was bombarded with texts. When could I bring the cat? I explained that it wasn't actually my cat, it was my cousin's and he had changed plans and just taken it on a trip to Lake Como. The landlady was obsessed. She texted again to ask when was the cat coming back? By now my mythical cousin had an elderly mother who was looking after the cat. She was very attached to it and couldn't bear to part with it. 'Freddy the cat' had increasingly preposterous adventures over the ensuing months, and it acquired a comprehensive backstory. The landlady was tenacious. Even after Freddy's tragic and untimely demise, the victim of a savage Great Dane let loose in the courtyard of the apartment building on Como by an irresponsible German owner, the landlady didn't give up. She was very sorry for my cousin's elderly mother, for whom, at eighty-nine, it had certainly been a dreadful blow, but was my cousin planning on getting another Ragdoll male? I blocked her number.

*

Together, Bee and I formed the Milan Chapter of the Martha Gellhorn Fanclub. We were the members. The club met once a fortnight at a Chinese restaurant near Bar Basso, where the Negroni *sbagliato* (mistaken negroni) was invented. The club's purpose was the discussion of all the ways in which we felt our careers were becoming adjuncts to those of our husbands, or as Martha Gellhorn herself put it, 'I've been a writer for over forty years. I was a writer before I met him and I was a writer after I left him. Why should I be merely a footnote in his life?'

The 'him' was Ernest Hemingway of course. As a general rule of life, it is unwise to trust any man over the age of twenty-five who claims Hemingway as his favourite writer. Bee and I might have lighted on any number of women to be the emblem of our club, but we shared a particular affection for Martha. She had gone on her first suffragette march aged seven and been fired from her first journalism job at the United Press Bureau in Paris for reporting one of her colleagues who had attempted to sexually molest her. Martha wrote about fashion for *Vogue*, and we particularly relished the detail that she had had the slacks she wore to report from war zones specially tailored by Saks, Fifth Avenue. Most of all, we chose Martha because of D-Day.

Martha first met Ernest in 1936 and married him in 1940. To us, the first years of their relationship sounded marvellous, a dream of complicity. They travelled together to Barcelona and reported side by side on the Spanish Civil War, though Martha later recalled that she began to have doubts during a bombardment when they took shelter in a house which was being shelled and Ernest and the other men in their group locked themselves safely in the cellar to booze and carouse, leaving the women and children exposed on the first floor. When the Second World War broke out, Ernest hightailed off to his ranch in Cuba, where he spent much time sailing up and down the coast, patrolling for non-existent German U-boats. Martha covered the conflict from Europe and Asia and was in England as what seemed like the biggest story of the century gathered force.

With D-Day approaching, she arranged for her husband to travel to Europe, wangling a place on a transatlantic flight for him with the help of an RAF officer named Roald Dahl. Martha described Ernest's reaction to their joint biographer, Berenice Kurt: 'Ernest begins at once to rave at me . . . my crime really is to have been at war when he has not, but that is not how he puts it . . . I am supposedly insane, I only want excitement and danger, I have no responsibility to anyone, I am selfish beyond belief.' That didn't stop Ernest taking the seat on the plane, or from deciding that he would file his copy, ultimately titled 'Voyage to Victory', for *Collier's*, the same magazine which employed his wife.

The five-page article includes a large photo of Ernest surrounded by a group of GIs. These men are gazing with delight and awe at the middle-aged, bearded man in their midst as though his presence matters almost more to them than confronting the Third Reich's last stand. 'The day we took Fox Green Beach was 6 June,' Ernest wrote. His piece goes on to describe how he went ashore, under heavy fire, from a thirty-six-foot landing craft, whose lieutenant he had already guided towards the correct spot, having strategically memorised the relevant landmarks. 'Once we waded ashore they began doing their stuff,' the article continues, positioning the writer right there, in the suck and spray of the surf and the bullets. Ernest didn't only land, he fought.

Martha did not land with the troops on D-Day though she was the first woman reporter to reach the site of the landings. She arrived in Normandy two days later, having stowed away on a hospital ship where she had spent the night locked in a lavatory. Women were strictly banned from reporting from combat zones, but as Martha explained to the soldier who interrogated her as she drove from London to the south coast of England to make her stowaway attempt, she intended to cover the women's angle. Since no one was interested in the women's angle it acted 'like the perfect forged passport'. Martha's article appears on page sixteen of the edition of *Collier's* which leads with 'Voyage to Victory'. It is one page long.

In the aftermath of the landings, Ernest travelled on to Paris as the Germans were fleeing. He claimed to have personally liberated the bar of the Ritz Hotel. Martha went to Dachau. When Bee and I formed our club, it was not widely known that no one had seen Ernest Hemingway thrashing through the water on to Fox Green Beach. No one had even seen him climb out of the boat, mainly because whilst the attack was underway he was offshore in a troop carrier named the *Dorothea G*. Now, a cursory Google search will elicit this information, but only if you're prepared to wade through pages of affirmations of Ernest's presence first. Martha's version has been publicised in an HBO documentary, where she is voiced by Meryl Streep. Back then we toasted Martha's memory over our chicken with bamboo shoots believing we were in the minority. We liked to think we knew what really happened.

*

I had to know if Anne Clarke was behind Giovanni Piccolo's attack. Bee had freelanced for several major Italian papers including the *Repubblica* and the *Corriere* and was now writing for *Wired* and other tech publications in San Francisco.

'So how do you want me to do it?' There was a beat after her voice; the transatlantic bounce.

'Message him now. Tell him you've heard he's involved in a potentially sensational court action and you'd like some background for a story. You understand the need for discretion but if the case goes his way tomorrow you'll lead the way with an exclusive. He'll have time to look you up overnight and see your byline.'

'You think he'll buy it?'

'Of course he will. He's desperate for attention, thinks he's a neglected genius. Get all you can if he talks, but the crucial part is why and when.'

'No problem, *ciccia*. Bad babysitters forever, right'

'Forever . . .'

*

Every afternoon, when I lived in Milan, I had taken my daughter to the park, sometimes to the Public Gardens, sometimes to the Villa Belgiojoso Bonaparte opposite. The gardens of the villa, with their pond and waterfall, were reserved for children, and there was a visible class distinction between the two parks. The Public Gardens had better play equipment and more space, but the rhododendron bushes rustled with tramps and junkies. There wasn't much for kids to do at the Villa, but the lawns were pristine, and if the weather was fine, well-dressed children and their mothers and nannies played on the neatly mown grass or sat around chatting. The diets, behaviour and illnesses of children were the sole topics of conversation. I was grateful for anyone to talk to, yet sometimes wondered whether the other women were as bored as I was.

Occasionally one of the mothers would organise a tea party at her home, in an apartment in a neighbourhood similar to the one in which I lived. Inevitably, the door would be opened by a uniformed maid. The guests were divided into two groups: nannies and children were in one room and given Coca Cola or orange juice; the mothers were in another room and served tea and Prosecco. The mothers had glossy hair, velvety skin and lots of jewellery. I wore scruffy jeans and beanie hats. Inevitably, the maid would show me to the nanny area. Sometimes the hostess would find me there amongst the quiet Filipina women whose own children were on the other side of the world. Sometimes I'd stay there for the whole afternoon, not liking to point out the mistake. I preferred it that way. My daughter played while I read my book and watched the quiet-eyed nannies. I wondered about their seething hearts. Yet when it was my turn to give the tea party I borrowed my mother-in-law's housekeeper and put on make-up and a cashmere sweater and arranged a row of chairs in the hallway of my apartment for the nannies.

Bee told me I was a hypocrite, which I was. I didn't want to give these women a reason to look down on me, even though I disliked what

I saw as their casual racism. In Milan 'Filipina' is still synonymous with 'female servant,' even though the woman in question might be from Peru or Moldova, and it was used unselfconsciously, in contrast to the mothers I knew in London, who called their nannies by their first names and pretended to be interested in their lives. Perhaps the Milanese women were actually more honest, I told Bee, in that they knew there was a class difference, and that difference was based partly on race. However reprehensible, they looked it in the face. I was also an inverted snob, I added, in that I prided myself on being genuinely aware of these women as people.

'You can add patronising,' said Bee.

What I couldn't quite tell her was that the Milanese mothers frightened me. Some of them were genuinely dull and stupid, yet many of them were not. They had degrees from impressive universities and some of them had held prestigious jobs before having babies, yet their conversation focused solely around their children. '*Bellissimo*' was a favourite adjective. I had read *The Feminine Mystique*, I knew that behind those clear eyes and fresh skins there probably lurked all manner of frustrations, yet they projected an air of incurious serenity which made me feel both angry and weak. I didn't want to be like them, and yet I craved their apparent tranquillity, their seeming sense of contentment in their world.

The apartments I visited looked very similar to my own, with their mixture of contemporary Italian furniture and a few family antiques — a mahogany sideboard, a worn nineteenth-century kelim. They were light and airy. Italian mothers seemed to be much better than English ones at keeping the depredations of children at bay — no toddler-high grub on the walls, no depressing heaps of garish neglected plastic. Silver was a major feature: photographs in silver frames, silver trays to serve drinks, artful little silver snuffboxes scattered about on modern glass tables. As a wedding present, I had received a silver Pyrex dish holder from some friends of my husband's parents. The ovenproof glass tray fitted into a silver-plated trivet with handles that could be brought to the table to serve, both elegant and practical. I saw many of those trays and whenever I did I thought of Sebastian in his empty flat in Soho, shooting up, making things, breaking things. I had the things, I had the ballast to fix me to the earth, but even a silver Pyrex dish holder didn't feel heavy enough. The Milanese mothers were convinced by their lives in a way which seemed entirely unattainable to me. I wondered what Emma and Polly and Lucy would have made of it.

*

Bee had turned up one afternoon at the Villa gardens with a coolbox full of beer cans. She smelled of the beer which had spilled across her duffel coat. She plumped herself down next to me and lit a cigarette even though she never smoked. Winking, she said, 'I thought I'd be your new nanny.'

The two of us stretched out on the grass and closed our eyes under the first warm spring sunshine as my daughter played with a tuft of dandelions. I thought I heard Bee begin a story about her journey to work in a loud voice, in perfect Pugliese dialect, guttural and studded with obscure blasphemies. In my dozy mind's eye, I saw the mothers staring disapprovingly as the famous Miss Stefanelli puffed on her fag and cracked a beer.

'Can I grab one?' asked Maria Vittoria's mother, or was it Maria Camilla?

'You know,' said Whoever's mother, 'sometimes you just think, *porca puttana*! I feel like a beer.'

Bee's eyebrows shot up over the top of her giant sunglasses, 'Er, sure. Help yourself.'

As the afternoon drew on, more mothers joined us. Bummed Bee's cigarettes. Went round the corner to get a couple of bottles of Prosecco. When there were no glasses left, one mother emptied out her son's Maisie Mouse drinking cup and swigged from that. They kicked off their immaculate shoes and wriggled bare toes in the grass. There were tears and commiserations as one wailed that she couldn't stand another weekend in the country with her in-laws. A Filipina nanny slid an arm around her shoulders. It grew colder, a thin blue breeze snaked down from the mountains, but no one wanted to leave. Astonished at the sudden window of neglect, the toddlers tweaked plaintively at their mother's sleeves for a while, then staggered off to hit each other and splash in the mud at the edge of the lake. When enough of them had started screaming, a mother produced a stash of Kinder bars from her Prada tote and stuffed them at their grimy, snotty little faces. Bee put on a playlist of Italian hits from her phone and as it grew dark the mothers swayed and giggled and slow-danced in a two-step to Adriano Celentano.

Bee did do the thing with the beers and the dialect, though the rest didn't happen. But bad babysitting was still pretty good.

*

By nine in the morning on the day of the hearing, I was already dizzy with nicotine.

Bee called from the middle of her night, 'I spoke to him. What a total fucking douche.'

'We know that. What did you get?' I had told Bee very little about Anne Clarke, and just said that I was convinced the weird anonymous emails I had received were probably from one of my lovers' wives. And that I needed to know if there was a link between them and Giovanni Piccolo — if he had been put up to suing me.

'He self-publishes his crappy book and gets zilch attention despite his deep research and passion for such an original subject, blah blah blah. He was so jacked about finally getting his name in the paper because of the case. I had to listen to a lot of hot air, he didn't want to reveal much. He thinks he'll be paid a fortune for interviews if he wins. Which he won't, doll. He's batshit, I promise.'

'But did he tell you why he started it?'

'He got an email signed "A Friend" via his website in the summer, roundabout the end of July, but was cagey. I didn't want to make him suspicious by interrogating him. He said it was in Italian, claimed your book was a copy of his and he should defend his artistic integrity.'

The two copies of *Lisianta* which had been bought in the UK had been sold in July and August.

'The email address?' I asked.

'He wouldn't say. But whoever it was could obviously have created a fake one just to send it. He said he didn't reply.'

I had been right: the idea of plagiarism had been planted in

Giovanni Piccolo's mind by someone who had read his book and noted enough superficial similarities with my novel to play on his conceit. Yet Giovanni Piccolo had admitted to Bee that *Lisianta* hadn't received much attention: how could Anne Clarke have found her straw man?

*

A text from my editor: 'We're going in. Speak soon.'

A few minutes earlier, Giovanni Piccolo had posted a selfie on Instagram from the steps of the courthouse, grinning up at the screen with his arm across the shoulders of his lawyer. The lawyer was in formal gown and hood, but I couldn't see his face as it was concealed by swirling emojis. Thumbs up. Fist pumps. Gloating over all the attention he believed he was finally going to receive.

*

I opened the file on my laptop desktop which contained the list of comparisons between my novel and Giovanni Piccolo's. Writers invariably use certain details for verisimilitude when describing the imagined lives of imagined people — my character ordered a drink in a bar and left the money on the table as did his, etc. Two things stood out: Piccolo's story was partly set in Paris and the heroine worked in the art world. I re-read the articles in the Italian press which had reviewed my book, nearly all of which mentioned the locations (London, Italy, Paris) and the fact that the heroine worked in an auction house.

I imagined I was Anne Clarke. What was her procedure to find a book that had striking similarities to mine? A European language for starters. I tapped 'auction house' into Google Translate, German, and up came *Auktions Haus*. Ditto for the word 'novel,' and up came *roman*. I then did a search using both words in German and added '+ Paris' and a phrase about my novel; then some references; and Amazon links to other books set in the art world. I repeated the same procedure in French and Spanish. Nothing in particular stood out. Perhaps Anne Clarke had emailed other writers of thematically similar books suggesting plagiarism, but they had more sense than Giovanni Piccolo and were not baited.

I typed in Italian, *casa d'aste* and *romanzo*. I scrolled through pages of links to Italian press reviews for my book, and on the fifth browser page, I spotted a link to the website through which Piccolo had sold *Lisianta*, and through that a link to his website. One look at that mincing selfie and I would have treated myself to a dry sherry. He might as well have had 'Mark' written on his forehead. Easy-peasy. Anne Clarke must have crowed with delight: it only took a few minutes to find Giovanni Piccolo and order the book. Then translate the whole thing online and email the author. It was just an afternoon's work.

*

That afternoon I was taking my daughter to the Christmas fair at the Swedish Church, as I did every year. We would eat cardamom buns and prinzess-torte with thick bright green marzipan, listen to the choir, queue up so she could plunge her hand into the bran tub to find a painted wooden horse or a tiny troll. Before we left, we would buy a Tomte, a bearded, gnome-like creature with a pointed hat and a round nose and take him home to sit in the hallway for Christmas. In Swedish folklore, the Tomte is a house sprite who lives in sheds and woodpiles and has to be appeased with a bowl of porridge every evening, lest he bring bad luck.

From my front window I watched a group of ladies arriving dressed in full dirndl skirts with puff-sleeve white blouses and embroidered bodices. By this afternoon, the court case would be over. All I had to do was sit and wait for news at the table where I had written the novel. The Swedish ladies bustled about, hanging blue and yellow bunting, positioning garlands of electric candles in the church windows. There was nothing on the table in front of me except my phone, positioned slightly to the right of my chair. I looked between the screen and the Swedish ladies until my agent's number buzzed up.

'Hi there. Can you take a conference call?'

Bad news then. I waited as, one by one, my Italian editor then my English publisher were patched in. The plagiarism case had been adjourned for consideration. The Italian judge had reserved the right to compare the two works in consideration of the list of textual resemblances. A date would be set for a further hearing, likely to be early spring.

We had proved that it was chronologically impossible for me to have copied Giovanni Piccolo's work. My manuscript had been read and sold long before *Lisianta* had been issued online. Given this fact, I asked why the possibility of my potentially having copied it was even being discussed? The timeline we had presented was clear, coherent and simple. If this had been a murder case, I would effectively have had an unbreakable alibi, yet for this the timeline had not been sufficient. Why had I not been allowed to talk to the lawyer who was defending my work? Why had I been discouraged from attending the tribunal when Giovanni Piccolo had been present? Why had I not been told which of the numerous documents we had compiled had been selected for presentation to the judge?

My Italian editor sounded exhausted and bored. He explained that this was a formality, that there was nothing to worry about. I pointed out that it wasn't his reputation and career that were being destroyed by the myopia of the Italian legal system. The suggestion of the merest possibility of plagiarism could cause severe damage not only to me, but to my publishers. How could I be reassured given this outcome? A short silence stretched across the plains of France, over the English Channel and across a couple of London boroughs. I vaguely heard the words, 'Don't worry and do try to have a happy Christmas.'

No one said it aloud, but the word *hysterical* hovered once more in the air.

16. SWEETIELAND

Along with the Swedish Fair and the Marylebone Lights, a performance of the *Nutcracker* was part of the Christmas ritual I had constructed for myself and my daughter. Our tickets were for two days after the inconclusive plagiarism hearing. When my daughter was back from school we prepared a small pink suitcase — I confess I got the idea from B — with our picnic for the interval. There were brioche rolls, thickly buttered, with rindless ham, sandwiches, thinly buttered, with cucumber and black pepper, miniature sausage rolls, small pink iced cakes of the 'shop bought' kind, which my own mother had only allowed as a special treat, and two bottles of pink lemonade with straws. I had also prepared a miniature version of the picnic for my daughter's doll Emmeline, and the suitcase contained a fat palm-sized red velvet cushion for her to sit on.

Emmeline was never to be referred to aloud as a doll, only as 'a small yet extremely sophisticated person'. She was an old-fashioned doll, the china-faced type, which I had bought after the divorce when we moved to our new home and became what the *Daily Mail* calls a single-parent-family.

Emmeline had arrived wearing a label attached to her muff, on which I had written in cursive handwriting:

Dear Miss-
I am Emmeline. I have arrived from Victorian days. I hope we shall have a lovely time together.

A chest of drawers in my daughter's bedroom was devoted to

Emmeline's possessions. Besides an extensive wardrobe of day, night and formalwear, she had tiny books, a tiny photograph album with real tiny photographs, furniture, a painting easel and a miniature harpsichord. When my daughter opened her stocking on Christmas morning, Emmeline had one too, with her name embroidered on it, filled with wrapped size-appropriate gifts with tiny ribbon rosettes. For the theatre, Emmeline and my daughter had matching dresses in black velvet with white collars. My daughter called it her 'Pauline Fossil dress' after the oldest of the three orphans in the Noel Streatfeild children's novel *Ballet Shoes*. I had a black velvet opera skirt and a cream silk blouse and we all wore Mary-Jane shoes with straps, mine with high block heels.

*

I did not find it easy to lose myself in the *Nutcracker*. All I could think about was Giovanni Piccolo. When I managed to stop thinking about him during the Christmas party and the duets in the Land of Sweets, or as we ate our picnic from the pink suitcase, I chided myself for being a fraud. The Sugar Plum Fairy was no match for the cackling creature inside me. Who was I trying to kid with my oh-so-perfect miniature cucumber sandwiches and my black velvet? Trying to 'build memories' for my daughter, to make her remember being little as a happy time, was as much for my benefit as for hers. Who was this performance for? All my attempts to make her feel special and safe and loved seemed staged, alienating, unnatural. If I could see through it all, one day she would too.

*

When we got home, the lock to the front door had frozen as it was intensely cold, more than usual for December. I couldn't get the key to turn. I jiggled and pushed, tried greasing it with lipsalve from my handbag, but it wouldn't budge. The Swedish Church across the street was lit up for a function from which a group of men in black tie had emerged for a smoke. I tapped across the icy road in my Mary-Janes and asked for help. One of the men crossed back over with me to see to the lock. In the light above the front door, I noticed that he was slightly drunk, swaying a little as the freezing air and the nicotine hit the alcohol in his system. A feeling with which I was not unfamiliar. He was quite handsome, or at least blandly privileged enough to appear so. He introduced himself as Daniel and gravely bent over our hands, including Emmeline's. His blond hair flopped in his eyes as he too struggled with the key, which wouldn't shift. My daughter's skin looked bluish. It seemed we'd have to check into a hotel for the night and call a locksmith in the morning, but then I remembered the hardware shop's emergency service for people living in the area. Mr Ali kept a master copy, and there was a helpline – namely his mobile – to call if you had lost your keys. Although I didn't like to disturb anyone so late, I took off my gloves and tried to squeeze some warmth into my fingers before tapping the contacts on my phone.

'Is there no other way in?' Daniel asked.

'No. At least, only that way, up there.'

I pointed to my bedroom window at the front of the building. The bottom sash was open an inch; this couldn't be seen from the road but I left it open a crack to let in a breeze. In my childhood home it had been usual to find ice on the inside of the windows on winter mornings, and I still couldn't sleep in a stuffy bedroom. Daniel looked around, then took off his dinner jacket and handed it to me. I put it over my daughter's shoulders. He was tall enough to reach the lintel above the door. As he hauled himself up until he could stand on the ledge, his wedding ring glinted in the streetlight. I was sure he would fall as he tried to open the window and couldn't look, but then I heard the grate of the sash and opened my eyes to see a leg disappearing into my bedroom. Seconds later Daniel let us in through the front door, enormously pleased with himself.

'I should offer you a drink, though I only have wine.'

'I should get back, please don't trouble. And you need to get these two young ladies to bed', he said, smiling at my daughter and Emmeline.

'I can't thank you enough. I don't know what we'd have done . . .'

'Take my number.'

'OK. But be warned, this house only exists for twenty-four hours in every year. If you were to come back after midnight tomorrow, you'd find it boarded up and abandoned.'

I don't know why I said that.

'You'd better call me tomorrow then.' Daniel stepped over the Tomte, seated placidly before his porridge. I chained the door.

Later in the night I came awake sitting upright, the muscles in my arms and legs cramping in knots of fluttering agony. I shouldn't have drunk the bottle of wine I had offered to Daniel. *Had* the window been open when we left for the theatre? I was turning into one of the women my agent had warned me not to write about, pissed and paranoid. I needed to get a grip.

*

Daniel returned to my house the next evening. Before he arrived, I took off my knickers and put a dessert spoon of powdered green cardamom on a saucer. I held my lighter against it until an ember began to glow in the middle of the spice, releasing the piquant, heady smoke. This was the perfume Cleopatra had reputedly burned in her rooms when she received her Roman lovers. The lamps were switched off; three tall green candles burned on the table.

Without speaking, without fully undressing, we had sex on the floor just inside the front door. I held him by the shoulders, slamming my body down on him until he came, then I climbed off and shook out my dress.

As he got to his feet, I stepped aside so that he could see the hall table where I had laid out a single crystal wineglass and my biggest kitchen knife, a steel Global, next to the candlesticks.

'You remember I told you that this house only exists for twenty-four hours in every year?'

'Indeed I do.'

'We have particular tastes.'

Daniel's eyes flicked between mine, the knife and the glass. I took a step towards him.

'Don't worry, it won't hurt.'

'Is this a game?'

I snarled at him, baring my teeth. He was out of the front door in half a heartbeat, leaving his overcoat on the floorboards. I watched as he ran away down the street and when he had disappeared round the corner I closed and chained the door and picked up the knife. It was a good one; my favourite: the weight in the handle allowed the tip of the long blade to be used with precision for tasks such as slitting the membrane inside a quail's egg just so.

I returned the knife to the block, filled the glass with red wine and drank it in the candlelight. It occurred to me that if my objective had been to have a man in the house to protect me from Anne Clarke climbing through the bedroom window, I hadn't exactly gone about it rationally. It was the kind of thing Sebastian might have done.

*

Christmas was spent at my father's house in Hertfordshire. There were five bedrooms, but with my sister and brothers and their families, it was crowded. A dormitory was made for the children in the attic; as the only single person I was given a brown corduroy sofa bed which had been pushed into the utility room for privacy. I went to bed between the washing machine and the ironing board, with the smells of dinner hovering from the kitchen. The ice machine in the fridge gobbled and gloated all through the night. In the article I had written for the *Tatler* magazine on how to be a good mistress, I had addressed the cliché of the lonely woman at Christmas, stressing that it was important not to be needy or whiny at this most depressing time of year.

H was at home in London with Lucy, B at home in Oxfordshire with Emma. F was in the cottage in Dorset to which he had moved with Polly after I threw him out. And here I was, twenty years after I had written that bumptious piece, alone on the sofa bed amongst the other utilities.

17. ACCEPTABLE IN THE 1980s

Before its playing fields were sold off at the end of the 1980s, the school I attended in the north of England had a reputation for sport. In other ways it was entirely average, but when I began there at the age of eleven it still produced some of the best junior athletes in the region. I had been selected to run the one hundred metres for the county so I was entitled to wear a special blue-and-yellow nylon tracksuit, of which I was extremely proud. I played in the netball and hockey teams and at one point was the national standing long jump champion.

The sports department was run by Mr Meadows and Mr Forge. On the day of the first games lesson, we lined up in the gym for a lecture from Mr Forge, who explained the Six S's: sporting success required strength, stamina, speed and suppleness. Then we were sent off to test our abilities on the cross country run, a looping route of about three miles which led out of the school grounds, up the hill, past the village church and back down to the school. Our times were noted by Mr Forge with his stopwatch and we were placed accordingly in different classes.

The girls' cross-country champion was Isobel Brown, two years above me. Every day at lunchtime she trained privately with Mr Forge and afterwards they would sit together in the school canteen to eat, just the two of them. Everyone was used to the sight. Isobel, who as well as being a good runner was very pretty, had an aura about her, a glow of specialness that came from being Mr Forge's favourite. After I had been at the school about a year, Isobel Brown gave up running and no longer ate her lunch with Mr Forge. She changed schools soon after for another large comprehensive in the next town. I sometimes saw her at the bus stop in her new green uniform.

*

During that year, when Isobel was still eating her packed lunch with her coach, Mr Meadows took an interest in me. I was learning to play the cello. Parents could rent musical instruments from the school to allow their children to try them out before committing to the expense of buying one, so every week I lugged in my cello in its hard, heavy case for my lesson. My parents lived very close to the school, just a few minutes' walk, but carrying the cello along with my books and games kit was a struggle. One afternoon, when the four o'clock bell had rung, I was dragging the cello through the car park when Mr Meadows stopped me and asked if I wanted him to run me round the corner. He put the cello in the boot of his car and drove me home. After that, he quite often waited for me on lesson days, to give me a hand.

A little while later, I stayed off school for the day with a cold. My parents were at work and my mother had left me a tin of Heinz oxtail soup for my lunch. I always wanted Heinz oxtail when I was ill, and my mother always had some just in case, even though she didn't approve of tinned food. I was heating the soup in the kitchen, still wearing my pyjamas, when a shadow passed by the window. The doorbell rang and there stood Mr Meadows. He asked me if my parents were at home, then explained that he had come to check if I was all right. Could he come in? It felt very strange to have a teacher in my home, but I knew the thing to do was to offer him a cup of tea, and he followed me back to the kitchen. I was embarrassed for him to see the tin of soup, I wished it had been my mother's homemade chicken-and-vegetable instead, but I made him the tea, and he sat next to me at the table to drink it. I didn't tell my parents that Mr Meadows had come round, not because he asked me not to mention it but because I knew, obscurely, that there was something wrong about it. Next week on cello day, there he was as usual, waiting for me. I didn't want to get into his car but I couldn't see a reason not to without seeming rude. After a few more lessons I told my parents that I was a useless cello player, which was true, and that I would like to try the flute instead.

People are much more conscientious about infections these days, but when I was at school mucus was something you put up with, like Mrs Thatcher. On a given day, half the class would be bubbling with cold. I didn't stay off school again until a really nasty bout of flu had my mother forbidding me to go in. Sure enough, Mr Meadows rang the bell at lunchtime. I stayed in bed with the quilt pulled up tight round my ears until my mother came home. All that afternoon, I had been terrified that I would hear his footsteps climbing the stairs.

I will never know if this was a test, but I have a feeling it was. Mr Meadows wanted to see what I would do, if I would refuse the lifts, if I would say something about the visits. When I didn't, Mr Forge asked if I should like him to coach me for the high jump. We had been practicing the scissor jump in class, where you kick your legs in a rapid one-two over the bar, but to be a real high jumper you need to learn the 'Fosbury Flop'. Named after the American Olympic champion Dick Fosbury, the move involves a curved run towards the bar, turning the shoulder towards it and arching the body over backwards, led by the arm. Jumpers can choose whether they make a right- or left-side take off. Mr Forge explained we would have to practice both ways to determine my stronger leg. The Fosbury also requires the jumper to lift their hips at the apex of the ascent to gain enough height for the legs to follow, so we would need to practice this too. It was the autumn term, and Mr Forge thought I had a good chance of a placing in the county trials in early summer.

*

Now that he was no longer running the cross country with Isobel Brown every day, Mr Forge had spare time at lunch. I met him in the gymnasium while the rest of my class was in the canteen. The girls' uniform for games was a white Aertex collared shirt with a blue jumper for winter, navy gym knickers with three white stripes on the side and a pleated navy games skirt. We were allowed to wear the skirt for netball and hockey, but for indoor activities and athletics it was compulsory to wear only the knickers. After a few laps of the gym to warm up, I lay on two thickly padded crash mats while Mr Forge put his hands either side of my hips and lifted them firmly a hundred times. Then we practised the run up, right side, left side (it turned out I was stronger on the left) and the leap itself, left arm stretched long to lead, knees together. Mr Forge lifted me and repositioned my body in the air at the correct angle.

After the training session there was just time to change and eat lunch. Mr Forge had an office behind the boys' changing room which was on the ground floor near the gym. The girls' changing room was upstairs, at the end of a long corridor. I changed back into my school uniform in the office, while Mr Forge talked to me through the door, then I ate the sandwiches from my lunchbox and he ate an apple. The office was dim, with a narrow line of windows at the angle of the ceiling and the whole place stank of sweat and mould and boys.

Naturally Mr Forge told me that I had to open my legs for the hip-flexing exercises. Naturally, the door of the office opened just a little wider every time. Naturally, Mr Forge said that it didn't matter if I was late for my afternoon lessons as I only needed to say I had been training. Naturally, none of my other teachers protested as I was never behind with my work and I was one of the school athletics champions. Naturally, I said nothing. And so it went, for the rest of the school year.

*

The county championships took place in June. Mr Meadows would drive the rest of the team to the track in the minibus, but I was chosen to get a lift in Mr Forge's car. I was always nervous before competing and Mr Forge wanted to ensure that I was as relaxed as possible. Nerves are good for running, the adrenalin loosens the fast-twitch fibres in the legs, but for jumping you need to be steady. The meet was scheduled to finish at 6 p.m., my parents had signed a consent form which said I would be returned to school by 7.30 p.m. The journey to the county town took a little less than an hour. I wasn't thinking about the bar or my technique or the competitors from other schools. I was thinking about those thirty minutes on the journey home, alone with Mr Forge.

It rained. The whole team was used to rainy meets and at first we waited around, shivering in our scanty kit, with the loudspeaker from the judges' stand announcing one ten-minute postponement after another. We did our stretches, drank water from miniature bottles. The drizzle became a downpour, the cinder track was red ice, the sandpits were flooded. The meet was called off. We would have to go back to school and return to our everyday lessons. Mr Forge was silent on the drive back.

I stopped doing athletics and refused to explain why, other than I was just bored with it. Then I stopped going to school. This was quite easy as my parents left for work before I set off. I would put on my school uniform, attend registration so that I was officially present and then simply walk out of the gates. No one ever challenged me and since there were a thousand or more pupils at the school it took a long time for the teachers to work out why I was seldom in class. I made sure to do my homework and stay in school on days when there were exams, but I spent the rest of the time at home, reading in my bedroom. It took another year for them to catch me.

When I was forced to attend school again, I started having sex with boys. I went to the family GP and asked for a prescription for the contraceptive pill. The pill made me very hungry: every day when I came home I would eat six slices of processed white bread with thick slabs of butter. My breasts swelled, my thighs thickened. I started smoking. A girl in my class who didn't like me told me she had overheard the chemistry teacher telling the biology teacher wasn't it a shame the Hilton girl had put on so much weight? Mr

Forge stopped looking at me.

*

With my daughter and my family in Hertfordshire, I went to a pantomime and the usual carol service. Emmeline came along, as did the cackling creature. I pulled crackers, wore a paper hat at Christmas lunch, watched the Queen's speech, played games with the children. And a fist of tears clenched tighter and bigger in my throat. It had to be swallowed down until I could reach the brown sofa every night, where I could stuff my head between the cushions and release it in gulping sobs that left me shuddering and breathless. My clothes were hanging off me, my skin was grey beneath the bronzing powder I applied each morning. No one is ever their best self by Boxing Day and nothing was said.

18. HAPPY FAMILIES

There were two things about my family's Christmas routine that always left me discomfited, moments that left me feeling desolate and ethereal, though I could never mention it.

My father had met his lifelong best friend Joey on his first day at grammar school in Liverpool. A boy at the back of the class had brought in a transistor radio. When the master asked who was singing, the boy said,'Sinatra, sir.'

'Well, stop singing at once, Sinatra.'

My father had loved Joey ever since, but as with most men of their generation they were undemonstrative in company. A clap on the shoulder in greeting was as far as their visible affection went. 'Keeping in touch' was mostly done by their wives, but at Christmas they rang each other up. Joey and my father both adored *Fairytale of New York* by The Pogues. It was their habit to have the song playing at both ends of the phone while they bellowed, 'All the best,' at each other. I had loved the song too, until Sebastian died. Shane MacGowan, the lead singer of The Pogues, had been a great friend of Sebastian's and they had spent several (what they called), 'brown Christmases' together, off their heads on smack. So that song left me feeling wretched, though we all had to crowd round the phone to listen.

*

Aged thirteen, my mother had been in the audience for the Beatles' first gig at the Cavern. My parents' teenage years had precisely spanned the time when nice girls from the South-East ran away from home to Liverpool, as once they had done to Weimar Berlin or the Parisian Rive Gauche in search of beautiful boys with bright red guitars in the spaces between the stars.

Along with Brian Patten and Roger McGough, Adrian Henri was one of the 'Liverpool Poets' whose Beat-inspired verse provided the literary counterpoint to the music of the Beatles when Liverpool had enjoyed its brief (and as it turned out moribund) efflorescence as the coolest place on earth.

My father and Joey worshipped the Beatles, but the Liverpool Poets came a pretty close second. During the Christmas phone call Joey would recite a poem by Adrian Henri, 'Talking After Christmas Blues'. I always thought it was a lousy poem, but these days it makes me feel nauseous.

*

My great-grandmother lived in an unusual house: an eighteenth-century cottage off Riddock Road in Bootle, on the outskirts of the city of Liverpool where the Mersey estuary becomes the Irish Sea. It was surrounded by streets of two-up-two-down terraces built for workers in the nineteenth century when Liverpool was one of the great ports of the world; their bleak brickwork, narrow backyards and outdoor privies had become an anomaly by the seventies, after Nazi bombs had seared through the dockyards and the council had erected cheap concrete and flatboard estates along the river's plain.

My great-grandmother's cottage belonged to the time before King Cotton reigned in the north of England, when the country was divided into landed estates. Though it was low-ceilinged and poky, it had been imagined humanely, with a front garden behind a low wall and a porch over the door where once, perhaps, it had been possible to sit at the end of the day and watch a pale sun glide down towards America.

There had been an apple tree there once, my mother remembered, and a Jack Russell named Patch. I asked her about my great-grandmother a good deal when I was eleven, in my last year at primary school, because I wanted to write a poem about her for a county-wide children's writing competition. My own memories were scant — the photograph of the son my great-grandmother had lost in the Second World War, a great uncle my mother had never known, the smell of the gas fire filling the 'front-room', the drone of the racing results from Aintree on the wireless. Physically, I had no recollection of my great-grandmother, who had died when I was five, but I imagined her as a little old lady dressed in black with spectacles and white hair in a bun.

That's boring, said my mother, and she explained to me what a cliché was. My great-grandmother hadn't been a little old lady with a neat bun. She drank Guinness and worked in a butcher's shop and was the heroine of the neighbourhood because she had 'The Sight'.

During the Second World War, when most Liverpool men served in the Navy, a neighbour had received the telegram informing her that her son was missing. His ship had been torpedoed in the Atlantic and no bodies had been recovered.

'Your great-grandmother heard the news,' explained my mother, 'and she put on her best hat. She went down the street and knocked on the neighbour's door. The kitchen was full of people trying to comfort the neighbour and making cups of tea.'

'Don't you worry,' said my great-grandmother, 'your George will come back right as rain. Just you wait.'

'How did she know?'

'Don't interrupt,' said my mother. 'She'd seen it in the fire, of course. And then a whole year later, George came striding up the street with his kitbag on his back, as right as rain. He'd been in the water for four days before a merchant boat picked him up, can you imagine? So then people began to ask your great-grandmother what was going to happen.'

'She was a witch?'

'Maybe. She didn't do magic, and she wouldn't read the flames for just anyone. She had what she called her casting days, and when she saw something she would go round to the person's house and tell them if it was important.'

I began to think about my great-grandmother's best hat and what people felt when they saw it coming along the street towards them. I added a bright red feather and a pale blue quilted brim.

'That's better,' said my mother.

*

Many years after the war had ended, my great-grandmother saw something so exciting in the fire that she ran outside without the hat. It was the day before the Grand National, the greatest and most perilous steeplechase horse race in Britain, and my great-grandmother had seen the name of the winner. She barged into the pub — in those days, my mother explained, women did not go into public bars, they sat separately, in the lounge bar, so this was a bold and disreputable thing for her to have done — and announced to all the men that the race would be won by a horse called Hayriver. The *Echo* newspaper was consulted, but there was no horse by that name amongst the runners. The men jeered at my great-grandmother.

'Ha,' she said. 'Mark you, green is unlucky. And Hayriver is the horse.'

Later that afternoon, as it was getting dark, there was a banging on the door of the cottage off Riddock Road. All the men from the pub were crowded into the porch.

Somebody was fond of the crossword in the paper and that somebody had listened to my great-grandmother and thought the name 'Hayriver' sounded like a clue. So he had fetched his special crossword-solver's dictionary and looked up the French word for 'hay' which turned out to be '*foin*'. There was a horse running in the National called 'Foinavon'.

'And the Avon is . . .?'

'A river. Exactly.'

Foinavon was an Irish nine-year-old and the odds were a dreadful 100/1. His trainer had been aiming to ride the race himself, but he was too heavy, so the owner looked for another jockey. Three riders turned the horse down and only three days before the race a man called John Buckingham finally accepted. He had never ridden a National before. None of this mattered to my great-grandmother's neighbours. They bet the rent money, they bet the dole money, they rattled the coins out of the gas meters and smashed their children's piggy-banks on the back kitchen tables. The next day, everyone who had a radio carried it to the front door so the street could listen.

What nobody except my great-grandmother knew was that when the race commentators had gone to the Aintree weighing room to familiarise themselves with the 'silks' – the jockey's colours – they found John Buckingham wearing black, red and yellow. Foinavon's silks were listed in the race card as green-on-green, but Buckingham sensed this was unlucky so at the last moment the colours had been changed.

Of the forty-four horses who start the National, twenty-eight remain as they soar into the second circuit. But Foinavon is at the back of the field, in twenty-second position. The neighbours are tense and angry. The horses are approaching the notorious Beecher's Brook jump: a fence nearly eight feet high set back a yard from the water in a wide ditch, with a 6ft 9in drop on the landing side. The two leading horses, Popham Down and April Rose are still running loose without their jockeys when Popham Down shies and races across the fence, panicking the followers. Seven horses fall, limbs and boughs and harness pile into a rats' nest of lethal energy from which the dazed jockeys fight free to remount, the commentators are screaming and the neighbours are silent and sick-faced but Foinavon is clear of the scrum, blinkered and confused, still running, when John Buckingham, bold young John Buckingham, slows to a canter and takes the fence. He looks over his shoulder, then he pulls out his crop and he drives the horse forward. The favourite, Honey End, is coming up fast, but John Buckingham melds his marrow with Foinavon's gait and they come in clear with twenty lengths to spare.

No one had ever seen anything like it.

My great-grandmother had not joined everyone outdoors to listen but had stayed indoors by her fire, smoking Player's Navy Cut.

The neighbours burst into the cottage and picked her up, armchair and all, and carried her on their shoulders round the streets.

'What happened then?'

My mother smiled. 'Well, your great-grandmother stopped casting after she got the gas, but she never paid for another drink in Bootle for the rest of her life.'

*

I wrote the poem and it won the county-wide competition. My parents were pleased, but they were far more excited about the judge who had awarded me the first prize: Adrian Henri. The headmistress of my school said that Caroline Jones should have won the prize as her handwriting was the neatest of all, but Adrian Henri told me that he had chosen mine because I hadn't tried to write about anything 'poetic'. He told the class that poems — in his Liverpool accent he pronounced it 'pomes' — should be 'true', which didn't mean beautiful or sweet, it wasn't flowers or kittens, but how something made you feel; that the poem was the agent for the writer's message. Later I learned that the Liverpool Poets were sometimes compared with Baudelaire for their insistence that what mattered about poetry was the effect it produced.

When he was signing the copy of his collected works that accompanied my book-token prize, Adrian Henri told me that I should look him up when I was a big girl.

*

So, seven years later, on my sixteenth birthday, I did. His name was right there in the telephone book and I dialled the 051 number from the landline phone — the only phone — on our kitchen wall. It seems improbably simple now, that one could do that: look up a number and call it and the person answered in their actual voice. But I did and he did and he asked if I should like to go and visit him at his home in Liverpool. My parents drove me to the appointment. They were to go for what it was still usual to call a 'Chinky' (which is horrible but that was how people spoke), and pick me up after I had had dinner with the great man.

Adrian Henri lived in a tall Georgian house near Liverpool Cathedral. On clear days you could see the cathedral tower just along the street from the nasty chintz armchair in my parents' sitting room. Perhaps Adrian Henri shook my father's hand on the doorstep. I don't remember and I could never bear to ask.

Aside from my own signed copy of Adrian Henri's collected works, there were several other editions of the Liverpool Poets in our house. Did my mother or my father remember reading Henri's poem 'Mrs Albion You've Got A Lovely Daughter (for Allen Gindberg)'?

Henri had written the poem after Ginsberg's visit to Liverpool in 1965, during which the American poet announced that 'Liverpool is at the present moment the centre of the consciousness of the human universe.' I had certainly read it, over and over again as December and my sixteenth birthday grew close.

The daughters of Albion . . .
Taking off their navy blue schooldrawers and
Putting on nylon panties ready for the night

The daughters of Albion . . .
Sleep in the dinnertime sunlight with old men
Looking up their skirts
[In the north of England, dinnertime was still midday]
. . . comb their dark blonde hair in suburban bedrooms
Powder their delicate little nipples
Wondering if tonight will be the night

*

When Henri told me to look him up when I was a big girl, he was fifty-two to my nine. When I telephoned him he was fifty-nine to my sixteen. I didn't own any nylon panties, but I had abundant dark blonde hair and had spent abundant time combing it in a suburban bedroom. Tonight was going to be the night. I was a daughter of Albion and Adrian Henri was going to take me on the dawn ferry to tomorrow.

The house was a little shabbier than I had expected, but it still looked very much as I expected a writer's should. Books and books and books, bright-coloured abstract paintings on the walls, a smell of old wine and tobacco, though that could have been from the cigarette I lit whilst swinging my legs from my perch on his scrubbepine kitchen table. Henri didn't fit it at all. He was big and fat, shambling and bearded, with thick lips and thick round glasses. His face had a questing air, like a thick-furred rodent, a coypu or a beaver. The kitchen was chilly and there were old spots of grease on the hob of the gas cooker. I don't know that we made much conversation, though I do remember that he told me he had a girlfriend. She was an academic and soon they would be attending the Christmas ball at Merton College, Oxford.

I told him that I was planning to go to Oxford. I wasn't scared of him. I didn't feel nervous or afraid. Reading his poems had taught me exactly the type of power I had over him and it thrilled me. I was legal and clearly, indisputably, unambiguously one hundred per cent up for it. His bedroom was even colder than the kitchen. The act was short and repulsive, as she had expected it to be.

*

A long time later, my mother told me that she knew what had happened that night at Henri's house. When my parents collected me, she said my hair was dirty. Beneath the door light of the family car, it shone with the dank grease of his hands. This was the only time either of us alluded to it. I didn't hear the word 'panties' again until I became B's slave.

19. HELLO, GOODBYE

Various things happened after New Year. The American firm who had contracted to publish my novels declined to release the final instalment. They said the central character was 'too unsympathetic'. So I would not be receiving the last part of the advance they had offered, which was heavily 'weighted towards the back end'. The character was precisely the same as in the first novel, the one they had bid for so aggressively, but there was very little my agent could do, despite the fact that I had honoured my end of the deal to the letter. There was a clause in the contract which gave them the option to cancel if the work was considered of an unacceptable standard. By that time the last instalment had been delivered to eight international houses, all of whom had accepted and indeed praised it, but this made no difference. Everyone said it was unethical and disgraceful and everyone said there was nothing to be done.

The reason behind the American withdrawal was that despite all the publicity elsewhere, the novel had been a flop in the States. Money and the bottom-line matter far more than publishers let on. There was a terrible review in the *New York Times* in which the critic described me as 'a quondam historian' who had 'discovered her inner babe'. One learns not to pay too much attention to reviews, good or bad, but this was especially frustrating, as the passages in the novel which the critic highlighted as being particularly awful had not actually been written by me. They were the work of my American editor, who had insisted I insert them. This happens a great deal — more than readers know. Since the Americans were the big payers, I hadn't been able to override the editor's 'advice'.

The Hollywood studio who had bought the rights decided not to make the movie after all. So I was broke again. Partly this was my own fault, because I'd spent the money I had earned like a sailor on shore leave, but I had 'hypothecated' the last tranche of the American advance to pay my taxes and leave a budget for living. Now I couldn't pay the taxes.

My agent had a proposal I had written for a new history book, with a draft for a potential TV drama series attached. I asked him to send it out for consideration as soon as possible. It was rejected over and over again. Eventually, one house did offer for it. The editor wrote a hugely flattering email in which she said she hoped to make me 'the new Amanda Foreman'. The financial business was inserted discreetly at the bottom: £15,000 for a book which would take two years to write. I did the sums and worked out that after commission I would earn £6,375 per annum if I wrote the book, before the tax I couldn't pay.

'It's the best you'll get,' said my agent. Since we were clearly no good for each other anymore we 'parted company'.

I wrote to several other agents, asking if they might take me on. The list included Horace Chisholm, the man who had been the agent for Belle de Jour's book. I hoped that perhaps Horace Chisholm thought he owed me a favour so I was prepared to humiliate myself, to go cap in hand to the person who had caused me such embarrassment and difficulty. He didn't reply to my enquiry and the others refused me. I had no American advance, no book contract and no agent. Effectively I was back precisely where I had started, except I was old and imminently bankrupt, with a legal case hanging over me and a child to support.

I was convinced that all this had to do with Giovanni Piccolo and therefore with Anne Clarke. Now as I lay awake at night I had someone new to curse. At 3.27 a.m. each morning I composed imaginary letters to my American editor in which I wished leukemia on her child and rot upon her womb. When I wasn't doing that I read the documents in the Piccolo case and Anne Clarke's emails over and over again.

Another email arrived in February with the first day of daffodil light:

Dear L.,
I daresay you don't give a damn but I believe we should all be responsible for whatever pain and grief we bring into the world.
Anne Clarke.

I similarly didn't give a damn any longer about hurting Emma or Lucy or Polly and wrote back:

So, Anne, Please could you tell me about the sliding scale of pain that makes you so morally fucking special? Has it occurred to you that there are some women who are so battered, so sad, that they just want to be hurt? Your husband grovelled on his knees when he told me that he couldn't be with anyone but me. Who is more to blame: him for swearing, or me for believing? Because, you see, I did believe him, for a while. Everything did seem new, clean, absolved. He made me feel rainwashed, luminescent, scrubbed shiny with love. He took apart a carapace I had taken years to build. Why don't you ask him about the pain and grief he has brought into the world? L.

This might have seemed a good moment really to commit to full-blown alcoholism. But I just couldn't find the discipline. Someone clever wrote that the best thing about being an alcoholic is that all you have to do is stop drinking and your problems are solved. However, that solution does require you to be a proper alcoholic first. If I had a hangover I couldn't hold anything sharp, even the kitchen scissors or my eyebrow tweezers, because all I could think about was how good it would feel to stab myself. So I couldn't have a hangover. Even the booze had given me up.

*

For my first history book, *Athenais, The Real Queen of France*, I had researched seventeenth century treatments for breast cancer, the disease which had killed Louis XIV's mother, Anne of Austria. She died horribly. The doctors made incisions in her breasts, into which they stuffed little collops of meat to 'nourish' the disease and counteract its devouring of her body.

That was what I was doing to myself. The creature inside me was cackling louder and louder, demanding to be fed with gobbets of pain. The more demanding it got, the more I crammed in, stuffing myself with regret and disgust and shame, and the greater its appetite grew, chattering and whispering constantly in my ears. I was a stupid, spoiled woman. Nothing so very terrible had happened to me, nothing that I hadn't done to myself, yet that knowledge was part of the creature's strength.

*

I found work at an events company. My job was making up copy to accompany 3D projections of museums and restaurants in which jewellery or fashion brands planned to spend hundreds of thousands of pounds feasting and entertaining influencers and high net worth individuals. It was quite enjoyable, though my thesaurus took a pounding on synonyms for 'luxury'. Another job was translating and editing the books of self-published writers, which was a fun irony. That paid quite well. I also pitched and wrote as many journalism features as I could, most of them about sex, each one a little morsel of sustenance for the cackling creature. When I wasn't at my writing table or trying to take care of my daughter, I crept about, looking for places to cry.

*

Having temporarily embraced sobriety, perhaps the thing to do was to try 'selfcare' and 'selfwork'. Meditation, yoga, baths with essential oils, wild swimming, a juice cleanse . . . I'd never gone in for any of that before, indeed I had spitefully aired my opinion that anyone who believed in the power of crystals didn't deserve the vote, but it seemed to work for other people. I was recommended a meditation app produced by a popular yogi called Sadh Guru. All I had to do to re-engineer my brain was to sit still for seven minutes, twice a day, repeating the mantra, 'I am not my body. I am not even my soul.' Had I actually believed I had a soul, what the fuck else was I? Wrong question. I looked up Sadh Guru and found a predictable history of dodgy contracts with the government of India's President Narendra Modi, luxury vehicles and an unproved murder charge.

I took myself to see a man who worked from a pleasant office in Bayswater, with dove grey walls and shelves full of pot plants. A large box of tissues stood on a table in front of a comfortable sofa, on which I sat to try to help the man to help me. It was the same maxi-size brand I had last seen discreetly positioned on my divorce lawyer's desk. Most of the tissues were soaked and used up after the half hour it took to explain about Anne Clarke and all that had led up to her. As I talked on and on between crying jags, the therapist began to look more and more disconcerted. He was dressed in black, with thick dark hair that kept falling over the rims of his fashionable glasses. I knew that somewhere in that soothing room would be a clock, discreetly positioned out of the patient's sightline.

'So,' said the therapist when I finally stopped speaking, 'had any interesting dreams lately?'

The remaining few minutes of our session passed in silence.

*

The plagiarism case returned to the Milan Internet Tribunal at the end of the month. Not only was it thrown out, but Giovanni Piccolo was fined several thousand Euros for 'temerarious litigation'. This ought to have put an end to my obsession with Piccolo, yet if anything I thought about him even more. I considered various gifts I might send him — flowers, a signed copy of my novel, a visit from

Pete the Gangster. Perhaps I should return to Sicily, to the small town in which his website declared he was so proud to live, and run across him on another smooth-cobbled street? Sicily, where I had bought the black notebook in which I wrote about 'Anne Clarke' and all my lovers' wives.

*

H rang me up, 'Have you seen the *Telegraph*?'

'Why would I have seen the Torygraph? That's your lot, not mine.'

'There's a piece. I'm sorry, darling, I thought I should warn you.'

A paragraph in the paper's gossip column was about me. The pretext for the piece was 'insider gossip' at a literary festival at a country house. I had not been at the festival. It quoted the Blonde Terrapin at the literary party who had said someone ought to throw a glass of champagne over me. She said that I was a 'dangerous woman'. The diary writer added that I was notorious for my affairs with married men.

*

Some days later B rang me up. 'Have you seen the . . .?'

'Whichever one it is I don't think I need to.'

The article he was calling about reported a rumour that 'easy-on-the-eye historian L.S. Hilton' was having an affair with a TV celebrity. Although it was untrue, it didn't stop B from saying, 'You really should be careful, darling,' in the kind of stern yet sorrowful voice a long-suffering friend might use to an incorrigibly childish adult.

B had not taken my defection from the Wine Press room well. He claimed to have attempted to kill himself in his Aston Martin by driving at 100 mph around the narrow lanes near his house at night with no lights on. When I said he was talking nonsense, he admitted to having worn his seatbelt. He cheered up when he found a new girlfriend. Though he did not confess to me that he had found another 'slave', I heard that he was seeing a woman named Marie-Chantelle. We grew friendly enough to speak again on the phone from time to time, and I even suggested that for Marie-Chantelle's sake he should go easy on the contraption.

*

Two more similar articles appeared in the gossip sections. F did not ring me up. My only contact with him had been through the vilipendious letter he had sent several weeks after I discovered that he had not told Polly that he wanted a divorce. On six typed sheets (single-spaced), he accused me of being a terrible writer and a worse mother. It interested me that F should know me so well yet so little. Telling me I was a bad mother was an absolute bullseye, but in all the time I had spent with F, I had never had any serious interest in his opinion of my work. According to F, my cynicism, cruel humour and lack of emotional engagement poisoned every page I wrote.

I hadn't loved F because I thought he was a nice person. As nor was I. We were unsympathetic characters. I could entirely understand

F being an unfaithful liar, a sociopathic compartmentaliser, a self-serving fantasist with ambitions beyond his no more than mediocre talent. I was those things too. Perhaps he had begun to find me ridiculous, as I had found him, but I did not think I was ridiculous. For all his peacocking, F ultimately lacked style, which was as shallow and unfeeling a reason to leave a person as one could think of, but there it was.

F had arrived at my flat with two large suitcases containing what he described as his worldly goods. In his hasty departure he had abandoned one of them. Shortly after I received the six-page letter, he sent a text asking if I would have the suitcase couriered to his club at his expense. I had been keeping it, planning to do just that, but after the letter I didn't want it in the house. I considered giving the contents to the charity shop in Marylebone High Street, but then I thought I might glimpse people walking around in bits of his clothing, so I put the case on the pavement for the bin men. The letter I burned. F had intended it to hurt me and I thought that this reaction was in some sense a compliment to his skill at invective.

*

Bee was delighted about the downfall of Giovanni Piccolo.

20. OUT OF OBSCURITY

After the articles came out I gave up. Anne Clarke had become a fixation. She had written to me of the intensity of her feelings, of her sense of vulnerability, humiliation and abandonment, and she had provoked those same feelings in me. She had watched me, followed me, read the mail in which I exposed my anger and pain. We were practically a couple. I wrote to her again:

Dear Anne,
I still have no idea who you are, but I accept that I have made you suffer. Perhaps you will believe me when I say that you have made me suffer too? Could we find a way to end this bizarre exchange? Perhaps you need to hear me say how sincerely sorry I am for the pain I have caused you. Tomorrow at three o'clock I will wait for you for an hour on the bench to the left of the pavilion in the Italian Gardens in Hyde Park. I hope that you will consent to meet me and that we can talk about everything calmly.
Yours respectfully, L.

I had given some thought to the time and place of the meeting. If Emma was coming from Mayfair she could easily walk or have her driver bring her. For Lucy, it was a convenient journey by Tube from North London. Or else for Polly, she would arrive by train at Waterloo station after a three-hour journey, hence I set the appointment for the afternoon, to give her time. I re-read the email, added 'truly' before 'hope' and pressed send.

Anne Clarke took several hours to reply. Her email consisted of one word: 'Fine.'

*

Once, perhaps, I would have spent abundant time considering how I should present myself for meeting Anne Clarke. Should I go counter-intuitively masculine in a blazer or suit? Or passive-aggressively youthful, barefaced in jeans and sneakers? Or live up to expectations in a trench coat, trilby and wistful expression? I no longer had the energy for role playing. I stayed in the same black sports leggings and baggy old jumper that I seemed to have been wearing for weeks, since my cascade of misfortunes had accelerated. I didn't even brush my hair. Anne Clarke had wanted to break me and she had succeeded. Maybe she would like to see my disarray. I had thought of saying I would be wearing a red scarf or carrying a copy of *The Times*, but we weren't spies. Anne Clarke knew what I looked like.

I was on the bench at 2.55 p.m. I was desperate to smoke, but that would make me look weak. It was a bright afternoon and the park was full of joggers and tourists. At 3.15 p.m. two riding instructors from the Hyde Park Stables riding school plodded past, their horses clipped to two child-size ponies on blue nylon leading reins, walking on in the direction of Kensington Palace. None of the passers-by looked like Polly, Lucy or Emma.

As I waited, I began to consider other candidates. Could Anne Clarke be the telephoning girlfriend from the apartment in Sicily? Could it be one of my own friends — Cathryn or Annabelle or even Bee, the kindly sleeper subtly referenced in an early aside who turns out to be the killer on the last page? As I had done long ago when

I began the black notebook, I began to list all the women I had potentially wounded; and all the men I had had sex with who might have had wives or girlfriends, year upon year.

The riding instructors came back. A young Asian man in a suit and tie sat down at the other end of the bench. I started, but he opened the *Evening Standard* while he ate a tuna baguette from Pret A Manger. The smell of the fish was nauseatingly strong, my mouth filled with saliva and I wanted to vomit.

'Excuse me?' I gulped.

'What?' and he took out an earbud. I hadn't noticed he was wearing headphones.

'Sorry, nothing. Sorry.'

He didn't get up to move away but his shoulders tightened as he briefly looked at me. Replacing the earbud, he took another bite of his sandwich. I was invisible to him, just one of those nutters who disturb people in the park while they were trying to get a few minutes' peace. I desperately wanted to explain, to tell him that I was waiting for an anonymous woman who was trying to ruin my life, to grab the lapels of his suit and cry into his white-shirted chest. What really frightened me was how close I came to doing that. At 4.05 p.m. I accepted what I realised I had known all along: Anne Clarke was not coming. She'd just been fucking with me a little bit more.

*

My daughter had a ballet lesson after school that day. She was getting a lift home with her friend Serena's mother, and they wouldn't be back until about six. The Marks and Spencer's food hall at Marble Arch was nearby. I'd get her a pack of prawn toasts for her supper. She loved them with sticks of cucumber and lots of salty soy sauce.

When I got back to my flat with the carrier bag, the front door was wide open. I told myself that I hadn't closed it properly, that it must have blown open, but I had a queasy feeling and just *knew*.

The front curtains were drawn, just as they had been when B came round in the afternoons. So this was how Anne Clarke wanted to play it.

'I'm here,' I called through the door, 'I'm coming in now.'

My reedy, nervous voice sounded ridiculous. What would I do next, tell Anne Clarke to 'show herself'? Find her lurking by the dishwasher with a Glock and defend myself with a packet of prawn toasts and a selection of dim sum?

'Oh,' I said out loud, and dropped the carrier bag.

The sitting room floor was covered with books: my books. They had been pulled from the shelves, shoved into chaotic heaps, some of them with torn covers and pages ripped out. My hands flapped uselessly at my sides. There was a high whining noise which after a few seconds I realised came from me. I began to gather the books and stuff them back anyhow on to the shelves. My daughter couldn't see this. Then I dropped my armful of books and walked through the house. It was empty, there was no one there.

When we had moved in, it had taken me two days to arrange my books correctly. I have a system: first they are grouped by period, then by genre, then in alphabetical order. Casting my mind over a mental map of the shelves, I could know precisely where to find Fielding or Auden or whatever volume I needed. It was 5.10 p.m., there was no time to put them back properly. I hung up my coat, washed my hands and set to replacing them on the nearest shelves from which they had been thrown, the only concession to order being that the spines faced out, otherwise my daughter would surely notice. I had to hurry, but first there was the door. The panels and frame looked normal, no dents or fresh scratches in the paint. The lock snipped on and off as it always did. No signs of forced entry. What did 'forced entry' even look like?

Assuming Anne Clarke hadn't slipped the lock with a credit card or a handy hairpin, she must have a key to my flat. I inserted my own key and the bolt slid smoothly in response. I'd bought some WD40 to loosen the lock after the night it had jammed after the ballet and Daniel climbed in through the window. My thoughts stopped on Daniel, who had never come back for his overcoat. Was this him, as a revenge for my idiotic vampire moment? So nothing to do with Anne Clarke? I had to sit down for a cigarette.

Then I saw it, a plain sheet of A4 paper lying on the table. In the centre was a note, and printed in neat italic capital letters in blue Biro:

PLEASE STAY AWAY FROM MY HUSBAND

Anne Clarke had been here. She knew I was going to be away from the house because I had asked her to meet me in the Italian Gardens. She had let herself in with a key. *Key. WD40.* I had had keys cut at the hardware shop: a spare for myself which was kept in that kitchen horrordrawer which everyone has — the one full of elastic bands and stray buttons and old takeaway menus. It was there. Also, a key for the babysitter and one for my mother to use when she looked after my daughter while I was travelling for work. I texted the babysitter and my mother to ask if by any chance they had mislaid their key? I continued shelving the books as quickly as I could. By the time Serena's mother's car drew up outside the room looked superficially normal and I had received replies from my mother and the babysitter. Neither of them had lost their key.

I ran round to the driver's seat. 'I'm so sorry, something's just come up that I have to deal with. Could you possibly stay with the girls here for ten minutes? I'll be as quick as I can.'

Without waiting for a reply, I sprinted off along the street. 'Do make yourself a cup of tea!' I shouted over my shoulder.

There were several customers waiting to be served in the hardware shop, but I pushed in front of them, panting. 'Mr Ali? Sorry, this is urgent. Remember I asked you to cut some keys for me? Did anyone . . . has anyone . . . have you cut one for someone else?'

'What's happened? Are you OK?'

'Please, just tell me if you made any copies?'

'No, of course not.'

'But you have the master copy. Where is it?'

'There are people waiting. I can look in a moment.'

'No. Look now. Because someone just broke into my fucking house, OK?'

'There's no need for language,' said a woman in the queue.

Mr Ali opened a drawer and removed a bunch of keys. He held a small one up towards me. 'This opens the key locker,' he said coldly. 'There is also a security code. Come with me.'

I followed him past the irritated shoppers down a narrow staircase behind the counter into the storeroom crowded with cans of paint, boxes of nails and screws. A worktable was piled with broken appliances, a high-backed dining chair wedged in beside it against the wall. Mr Ali climbed on to the chair and punched four digits into a keypad next to a metal locker. It was painted the same dull green as the walls, you'd have to know it was there to see it. The keypad buzzed and Mr Ali turned the small key to open the door,

'There,' he said.

Peering into the locker I saw rows of keys on hooks, arranged under taped labels with street names and then numbers. The key to my house was hanging there.

'I'm sorry, I'm really sorry . . . I didn't mean to suggest . . .'

Mr Ali ignored me.

*

'Is everything all right?' asked Serena's mother when I got back to the house. The girls were upstairs in my daughter's bedroom. She was standing too close to me. She wasn't really concerned; she was trying to see if I smelled of drink. I knew I looked as though I would smell of drink.

'Fine, all fine. So sorry to have held you up, it was very kind of you to stay, thank you.'

I was certain Serena's mother was thrilled to see me losing it. In my daughter's class at school, I was the only divorced parent. Yep, the freewheelin' single mum, the one who wrote about sex in the newspapers and had her name in the gossip columns in connection with married men, but was too busy with her 'career' to accept her responsibilities at the Summer Fair cake stall, that was me. Serena's mother's husband was called Thomas. He worked in advertising and had once put his hand on my thigh under the table at the parents' end-of-year lunch and asked me if I ever felt lonely. I wanted to tell Serena's mother that she could fuck right off with her fake empathy and her Red Velvet cupcakes. I wished I'd given Thomas a Chinese burn. Ha! Perhaps she was here, right under my nose. Anne Clarke was Serena's mother! I could take the scrunched up sheet of A4 from the fanny pocket of my sporty leggings and demand a confession!

'We must have Serena to tea after ballet next week,' I beamed.

'Are you all right, Mummy?' asked my daughter when I had finally, finally closed the front door.

'Of course, darling. Just had a bit of a stressful day with work. D'you want to sleep in my bed tonight?'

'With Monkey?'

'Of course.'

'And Emmeline?'

'Why don't you put Emmeline's bed in my room? I don't think she would care to share with Monkey, do you?'

*

Anne Clarke would not strike again tonight, besides even with a key she wouldn't get in with the chain on. While my daughter dressed Emmeline in a white frilled nightgown and bonnet ready for her sleepover, I called the divorced man who had been my occasional companion when I was travelling round the world to promote the novel. He was Danish. He lived in Copenhagen and owned a second house near Skagen to the north of the Jutland peninsula. We had not seen one another for a while; since we had never been in love we hadn't had to fall out of it, and we kept in touch with occasional text messages. If we could, we did each other the occasional favour — he had helped a friend with a job contact, I had lent his daughter my Saint Laurent silver cocktail dress for her school prom. I rang him up and asked him if I might borrow the house near Skagen.

The house was empty at that time of year, my ex-lover said, so I could stay there as long as I wanted. He gave me the address of the housekeeper in the port and kindly said he would call him to switch on the heat and make up a bed for me. Was I writing something?

'No, I'm staging the exposure of one of my ex-lovers' wives who's been stalking me,' was what I wanted to say, but said instead, 'That's it, yes. I have to meet a deadline.'

*

I had been to Skagen with the Danish man only once. We had driven from Copenhagen in early autumn, through hours of flat golden fields. The house was made of wood and glass and was full of sky. He cooked dinner for me, steak and wild mushrooms and a tiny dark purple berry that I had never eaten before under a crust of thick cream. I was meant to catch a flight from Aalborg back to London the next day, but I never got round to it. It was hot, we walked on the beach and swam and then lay under a willow tree in the garden, the shadows of its pied leaves like blue fish across our faces as the plane I had been meant to catch trailed curds of cloud above us. We laughed a lot. I was glad to have that memory.

*

I rang my mother and asked if my daughter could go to stay for a few days. I invented a conference in Oslo I'd been asked to join at the last minute which my publishers were pressuring me to attend. Not that I was going to Oslo, but it was near enough. We agreed that she would collect my daughter from school the next day and take her back to the country for a week. I emailed the school to say that I had been called away and that my daughter had to go to her grandmother's, after which I packed a bag for myself and one for her and booked the 12.20 p.m. flight to Aalborg from Luton. My daughter was thrilled at the plan of an unexpected visit to granny. We ate the prawn toasts in my bed, getting soy sauce all over the duvet. Emmeline had a sliver of toast on her breakfast tray, sitting up straight with her bonnet tied in a bow and looking most superior.

*

My next email to Anne Clarke said:

Dear Anne,
You've made your point. Enough. You know where I live. I am leaving instructions for you. You can find them underneath the aluminium pot to the right of the front door. Follow them. You have five days. After that, I will go to the police and I will prosecute you. Moreover, you will find your actions have had a serious effect on the lives of

several other women.

L.

A return ticket to Aalborg cost £79.00 with Ryanair. There were about 800 pounds left in my account, but this was not a moment for economies. I withdrew £300.00 from the cashpoint (feeling more grateful than ever for the whirring noise) to include the flight and taxis. Emma and Lucy would certainly be able to cover the expense, but perhaps not Polly; that is if either of them was in fact Anne Clarke at all. It was only polite to reimburse her expenses.

*

Had it not been for my family, I might be going to Skagen where I had once been so happy to kill myself. Though had I been genuinely suicidal, happiness would not have been a consideration. I just wanted to be in a quiet, remote place which had no connection with F or B or H, and England was too small. Everywhere I had thought of seemed to have some resonance for my lovers' wives – Emma was from Norfolk, Lucy and H had friends in Northumbria, Polly had spent family holidays with F in Devon. Whilst I knew so much about them, there were still so many memories, associations, impressions to which I was not privy that unless I chose to try to meet Anne in Croydon or Maidstone, I couldn't be sure of a location which would feel neutral. Only Danes go to Skagen. The Romans thought it was the end of the earth, where the world stopped dead and the seas were governed by monsters who had exchanged eyes for malice.

*

I put the money for Anne's journey in a plastic freezer bag and tucked it into a brown envelope. On one of the remaining blank pages in the black notebook I wrote the details of the daily flight, instructions for the taxi driver and the address of the house. Underneath that I wrote:

Meet me as directed within five days. I may have caused you to suffer, but your recent behavior is criminal. Stalking is an offence. You have broken into my home and damaged my property. If you do not show yourself, I will have no choice. I will go to the police, I will expose you and I will prosecute you.

When I tore it out to add to the envelope of cash, the page left a rough seam in the notebook along which I wrote 'Page removed for note to A.C.' I had to be out of the house in fifteen minutes if I was to make my flight so I called a cab.

The aluminium plant pot was heavier than anticipated. I was still struggling to lift it high enough to hide the envelope underneath when the cab drew up. The driver honked his horn impatiently and as I stood up to wave to let him know he was outside the correct address the pot fell back, trapping my foot. Swearing and hopping, trying not to fall over my bags, I spotted a woman in a long coat and headscarf on the pavement near me. At first I thought she was offering to help, but she just stood gawping.

'Yes?' I hissed and she scuttled away.

The cabbie glanced pointedly at his watch and opened a

newspaper as I struggled with the heavy pot.

*

I landed in Aalborg at 4 p.m., just as the sun had gone down. The short walk across the tarmac to the terminal reminded me of that genuine Scandinavian cold; a chill so raw and deep that it feels like an element in itself. I bundled myself into a taxi, gave the driver directions to the housekeeper's house in the port and asked him to wait while I fetched the keys. We stopped again so that I could buy some groceries at the implausibly clean supermarket, then drove out to the house. Once the taxi had gone I looked into all the rooms. The master bedroom where I had once slept in the Danish man's arms was made up, but I took the bedclothes and towels up another flight of stairs where I remembered there were two small bedrooms either side of a landing which gave on to a balcony overlooking the sea. For an hour or so I was busy, unpacking, looking through the kitchen and closing doors.

The front door opened from the direction of the road. The kitchen was on the right-hand side, a sitting room on the left. Both rooms ran the full length of the house, where they gave on to a third, set perpendicular, a living-dining space with one wall made entirely of glass, facing the beach. I closed off the doors at either end of the living and sitting rooms with chairs under the handles, then did the same with the main bedroom, second bedroom and study on the first floor, leaving access only to the upper rooms and the kitchen. I would have to walk outside and around the house to get to the beach, but this made me feel in control of the space. I knew there was a sauna hut in the garden but I wasn't going to go there in the dark. I felt too weak to light the kitchen stove and cook dinner. I locked the front door and made a cup of ginger turmeric tea from a jar of teabags. While it cooled, I showered in the small bathroom off the bedroom I had chosen and took two Zopiclone with water from the tap.

*

The tea was cold when I woke up. My phone told me it was five past ten; I had slept for fourteen hours. I texted the Danish man, thanking him and letting him know all was well in the house, then drank the tea sitting up in bed, from where I could see nothing but the waves and the sky. The house was deliciously warm, and it was an effort not to sink back into the drowsiness of the sleeping pills, but the thin draft of ozone sliding in through the inch of open window called me. I pushed myself out from under the duvet, put on my boots and two sweaters under Daniel's heavy overcoat and went for a long walk on the beach. In September the sea had been tinted a strange verdigris, but now it was pewter, with huge breakers thumping the shore. The silvery pale sand was the same though, gathering in my eyelashes and the folds of my scarf as I turned my face to the wind.

*

My father had once had a minor operation for a fairly rare condition named Dupuytren's disease, which causes a finger, usually the little one, to bend over crookedly like the top of a question mark and stay stuck. It is easily corrected under local anaesthetic. As the hand surgeon was slicing through the warped tendon, he remarked to my father that Dupuytren's disease afflicts only people with Viking DNA. My silverblond, ice-eyed father told me this with some surprise. It felt cool to know I had Viking blood.

Watching the surf, I thought of Philip Marlowe, standing on the edge of his soiled continent, recalling that once there had been "a clean open beach where the waves came in and creamed and the wind blew and you could smell something beyond hot fat and cold sweat". The few trees which grew along the beach at Skagen were shaped like my father's finger, crone-backed, bent low to the turf. Their branches reached horizontally forward, inland, clinging to their few inches of gritty purchase. Despite the brutal wind and the shattering winter storms, they were still there. They grew. Which was nice for them. I turned round and stumped back along the beach to wait for Anne Clarke.

21. TARTS

I did not expect Anne to arrive that first evening. In fact, I wondered if she'd come at all.

Emma, Lucy and Polly had families, commitments which would need to be rearranged to accommodate a sudden journey. It'd be a different matter if she were, say, a lone literary stalker. It was possible that whoever Anne was, she would take the four o'clock flight which landed in Skagen about six, so I had to be ready. The sauna house was padlocked. I felt reassured. Anne couldn't skulk about there. I closed all the blinds in the house and switched on all the lights, so even if she tried to peer in she wouldn't know which room I was in. She would have to enter by the front door: I wanted to see her before she saw me. The kitchen door opened inwards, making a blind spot to its left, opposite the wood burner and a dresser filled with blue and white Flora Danica crockery. I pushed a comfortable armchair behind the door, found a mop in a cupboard of cleaning equipment and propped it upright against another chair in the hall, to stand in for Anne Clarke. I had to open up all the bedrooms again to find what I needed next, a free-standing dressing table mirror. After I had closed them, I moved the plates from the dresser and tried the mirror in various positions until it was possible to see the mop in the hallway whilst sitting in the armchair behind the door. I felt quite pleased with this bit of stage business; it was the kind of thing the heroine of my novel got up to when she felt a murder coming on.

*

On the kitchen worktop I laid out my evidence, the black notebook, the single-sheet note from Anne, printouts of the legal documents from the Piccolo case, four newspaper clippings pinned together with a paper clip, the proofs of my version of events. Anne was likely to have many questions and I would answer them as clearly and openly as I was capable of doing.

I also had to think about weapons. Not that I believed Anne was physically aggressive, but I couldn't be completely unprepared. What if Anne was just a crazy, not one of my lovers' wives at all? Would a couple of kitchen knives down either side of the armchair do the job? Or else a heavy jug on the floor to grab, or a wine bottle to throw at the head? The Danish man had a nice collection of Gaia in a temperature-controlled rack next to the sink. Maybe the thing to do would be to drink the wine and use the empty bottle? I also checked the number for the Danish emergency services: 112. All set for my very own Nordic Noir.

I wasn't hungry even though I hadn't eaten anything since snatching a banana the previous morning. I felt faint and dizzy, which was nothing new. I forced myself to heat up a can of soup and ate it standing up, dunking a bread roll and surveying my stage set. There were steaks and salad and a pot of dill sauce in the fridge, a pack of smoked eel, pickled cucumber. And two individual ramekins of *crème brulée*. If everything went well we could enjoy a proper dinner together.

*

In the article I had written about 'my cheating career' when my daughter was a baby, I had described the particular pleasure of being temporarily absent from the world, when no one except your lover knows where you are.

At ten to six I unlocked the front door, then settled down in the armchair in the kitchen with a blanket over my knees and my copy of Nancy Mitford's *The Pursuit of Love*, one of a set of her collected novels. I had got through most of it again on the plane. Alone in that house at the end of the world I felt that pleasure of absence once again, knowing that Anne was coming to me and that we were the only people who knew it. Time was viscous, the minutes dripping by slow as amber through bark. The steady rustle of the pages and the shifting of the logs in the stove were the only sounds. It was peaceful.

*

Looking back on her relationship with Ernest Hemingway, Martha Gellhorn wondered whether she was responsible for his numerous infidelities. She was, she supposed, 'lousy' in bed. The only pleasure she had ever taken in sex was that of being wanted, being desired, the brief potency of being the object of a man's urge to possess.

I remembered sitting amongst a group of girls at university, consoling a friend whose boyfriend had just broken up with her. Everyone smoked in those days, the small student bedroom reeked of tobacco. The girl who had been dumped had wept until her eyes were so swollen she could hardly open them. There were five or six of us, sitting in a circle on the thin grey regulation-issue carpet, reaching out to touch her, patting at her arms and shoulders as she howled, whilst trying not to blow fag smoke into her poor eyes.

'I wouldn't mind,' she said, 'except I woke him up every morning with a cappuccino and a blow job.'

'You mustn't blame yourself,' someone said. 'You did all you could.'

Everyone agreed that she had done all she could.

Being 'good in bed" was of paramount importance. We were eighteen, nineteen, twenty, and we did all the things the magazines instructed us to do. We did oral, anal, reverse cowgirl, spanking, blindfolds, we sucked and we swallowed, we exercised our pelvic floors. In the future, when men carried porn in their pockets all the time, we would accustom ourselves to being spat on, having our hair pulled and being choked, and we would apply ourselves to these activities with the same diligence with which we went to spin classes or dyed the roots of our hair. It was no big deal, just one more component of being attractive. If like Martha we took no particular pleasure in any of this, we doubted ourselves because we had been taught that what men really want is to please their partners.

We believed we were free to control and enjoy our bodies but what that came down to was that we had to be pleasing in every possible way. The magazines told us that men were desperate to satisfy their women. What a crock. Men did what they liked, or at best what they believed we would like. Either we liked it or else we faked it, because 'frigid' was about the worst thing you could be.

*

Sebastian adored being photographed; he adored any kind of publicity. There are quite a few pictures which date from the first years of my friendship with him, when we were both writing for *The Sensualist*. In one, I am lying on a bed wearing the double-breasted jacket of Sebastian's pink suit, and in the companion shot he wears the suit trousers, caught in mid-air as he jumps on his reinforced bed. The magazine did an issue devoted to 'Gods and Godesses', for which I posed on the cover, a hand across my breasts, my lower body wrapped in a silver sheet. Inside I wore a pink coat and riding britches, supposed to represent a version of Diana, the goddess of hunting. The pictures had been locked away in my trunk after Sebastian's death but I think that shot featured the Global, standing in as a hunting knife. On the opposite page, the chef Gordon Ramsay posed as Vulcan, with both hands plunged into a huge lump of raw meat. Sebastian and I were reclining again for *Tatler*, me on a chaise longue, he once more on his bed. If you didn't know, it looked as though Sebastian's red-painted flat was a sumptuous place, but in fact it was quite stark and bare, with nothing remarkable in it except him.

After Sebastian died, a journalist wrote about knowing him, disclaiming any close relationship as he was not 'a member of that gilded inner circle', but very much in awe of his 'rapacious, unmatchable and seedy glamour, both distasteful and strangely exhilarating'. I too had been ensorcelled by those qualities, but I had never thought of myself as belonging to an 'inner circle'. Perhaps I did. Perhaps I didn't. I was in no doubt that our friendship was far more important to me than it was to him. I never lied to him, but he lied to everyone.

We often dined together at the Ivy (practically the only place where Sebastian could bear to be seen ingesting food) and sometimes afterwards I went with him to visit a prostitute in Shepherd Market. Sebastian was obsessed with prostitutes, an obsession which had become a significant part of his self-fashioning. Usually I waited outside with the maid while Sebastian had sex with the tart.

The kind of working girls Sebastian liked had mostly been driven out of Soho by gentrification. They belonged to a lost world of lamps draped in chiffon scarves, handwritten signs reading 'Model Upstairs' and fivers on the mantelshelf. The services they offered were as quaint as their surroundings — you paid extra for 'French', which was a blow job with red lipstick. As you climbed the stairs to their flats, the smell of bleach and cold tobacco gave way to the tinny rose of knock-off Hermès Calèche and Yardley talcum powder, the scent of a lost England, the one that according to Philip Larkin came to an end in 1963, pinched and grubby, an England still on rationing, where sex was furtive, shameful, joyless, prim. I thought that what appealed to Sebastian in all this was not erotic pleasure but the lack of it, the almost ascetic atmosphere of the ritual, the palefleshed girl, the thin towel, the piteous hiccup of slime on the greyed sheet.

Old-fashioned prostitutes always had a maid to receive the customers. What impressed me about both the girls and the maids was quite how ordinary they were. The maids were older, but otherwise there was no particular distinction between them. They looked like all the women you saw all over London, every day, there was nothing about their appearance or demeanour to suggest that their working lives were so extraordinary, so beyond the limit of many people's experiences. As I waited down below in the chilly, shabby flats I would notice little domestic touches: a bunch of artificial flowers, a sequinned cushion or once a ball of knitting, the needles stuck in a navy-blue scarf. There was nothing particularly gilded about any of it. Perhaps from the outside it might have seemed glamorous to know Sebastian. For me, the outings and the photographs were another part of our conversation, our complicity. Sebastian had the gift of making people feel chosen, yet however much I loved him I knew better than to believe he reserved it for me.

For much of the time that I knew him, Sebastian was working on his book, an autobiography. He wanted to call it *Mein Camp* but the publishers wouldn't allow it. Compiling the book — Sebastian was the first to admit to being a shameless and highly talented plagiarist — was a huge effort for him. As deadlines were pushed back and back again, he compared himself to the Count of Monte Cristo, 'at least that fucker got out eventually'. It came out as *Dandy in the Underworld* and it is a little masterpiece. The book was turned into a play, with the actor Milo Twomey to star as Sebastian.

As the opening night drew near, Sebastian sent a group email:

Hello, darlings,

You will find nothing wrong with this play -- except its appalling choice of subject.

I will drink and I will take drugs and in my weaker moments I will eat, but I will never, ever, go to a theatre.

Why would I go to a theatre to see rape, sodomy and drug addiction? I might as well stay at home.

Not true. You realise all people will be saying every night is:

'Who's that cunt on the front row with the top hat on? I can't see a fucking thing.'

A first-night party was being organised at a club near the theatre. I had volunteered to liaise with the caterers and had been particularly pleased to track down some poppy-scented incense, which I planned to burn at the entrance for an opium-den atmosphere. I recall having a conversation with someone about macarons, bright red, raspberry-flavoured macarons sprinkled with edible silver sparkles, to recall the scarlet-sequinned suit Sebastian had made for him in Savile Row and which the actor playing him would wear as his final costume.

*

Ten days or so before the play, the woman with whom my mother had fallen in love after she and my father divorced, and with whom she had lived for over ten years, was taken to hospital in the last stages of breast cancer. My sister and I went to the country to support our mother and wait for the end.

My mother's civil partner — we could say 'wife' now — died a few days later at the age of fifty-three. The funeral was set for the same day as Sebastian's play. I called him early in the morning to say I wouldn't be able to be there. Then I went out to pick wildflowers for the church. It was June and the fields were full of poppies.

When I returned to the house, there was a message from Sebastian. I knew exactly how he looked, speaking into the receiver, but his voice surprised me.

The message he left was: *'No, L. Say it ain't so. Say it ain't so.'*

I would listen to that message many many times in the months that followed. I could never know, but Sebastian's voice sounded as though he was in horrific pain, struggling up from somewhere I hoped never to have to go. If I had told someone, called someone, said that I thought something was wrong, perhaps he wouldn't have done it. But maybe I was trying to cling on to something that had never been there, the belief that I was special, that he needed me. I wanted to believe that, yet equally, if it was true, I had failed him.

My mother was stiff with grief and tranquillisers. She had applied a pale foundation, so thick it looked like putty, to keep her countenance. The morning after the funeral I went back to London. I had a day free before collecting my daughter to return to my mother's house. That afternoon, I had gone to the hotel in Park Lane where I had arranged to spend the afternoon in bed with H.

*

Sebastian died of the overdose of heroin just as the play about him opened. His death attracted a lot of publicity. People who had never met him debated whether it was suicide or an accident. Others claimed that he had faked his death and had been seen in Hull – he despised the place where he was born but that at least had the ring of an authentic Sebastian double bluff. The consensus was that when he shot up after the performance, having been clean for a while, the shock to his system killed him. This theory was supported by the fact that he left no note. Everyone agreed that it was entirely out of character for Sebastian to have resisted the opportunity to have a last word.

One of the writers to whose work I had introduced Sebastian at our tea parties was Jean Rhys. I gave him the novels, and we read some of the short stories together. We used to say in chorus the last lines of one, a story about a woman who shoots herself in a Parisian restaurant: 'Salut to you, little Russian girl, who had pluck enough and knowledge of the world enough, to finish when your good time was over.'

Perhaps Sebastian sensed what was coming: Instagram, Snapchat, Facebook, Tik Tok, the infinite vulgarities of social media, the insidious invasion of every moment of our lives by phones and posts and screens. He wouldn't have been able to resist the attention, was already ineluctably drawn to it. There is a video of him on YouTube: 'Sebastian Horsley's Guide to Whoring'. It is horrible. Sebastian is a scarecrow pastiche of himself, a preening clown. Privately, I disagreed with the people who thought that Sebastian could not have meant to die because he left nothing behind. He was naked when they found him, his suit and top hat laid to one side. Writing a note would have been to continue the performance. It was out of character, but then so was he.

*

Prostitution is legal in the Australian state of Victoria. During the one night I spent in the city of Melbourne, I decided to rent a male whore. I was curious as to how the procedure worked, and I found the idea exciting. What did male prostitutes call their johns – 'janes'? As a customer I would be entirely in control.

My English publisher was accompanying me on this stage of my promotional tour. We spent the day with journalists and booksellers, after which there was to be a dinner with a focus group of readers in a restaurant not far from the hotel. It was scheduled to end at 9.30 p.m., so during the hour I was given to change before engagements, I booked the prostitute to arrive at 10 p.m.

I quickly showered and redid my makeup ready for the dinner, then sat down in my hotel dressing gown to look at various escort agencies on my laptop. There were no pictures of the sex workers and appointments had to be made by phone. I chose the agency with the highest prices because I figured they would have the best-looking men. My call was answered by a nice-sounding lady who asked me to specify my requirements. I said I wanted a tall, fair-haired man, no older than thirty, with broad shoulders and a slim waist.

'Surfer type?' prompted the lady.

Exactly. He was to wear a white shirt and jeans, though I didn't mind a jacket if it was chilly.

'Let me see,' said the lady. 'We're quite busy this evening. Yes, you can have Zaveer. I think you'll like him. How long do you want? The minimum is ninety minutes.'

I said two hours.

'Do you want a boyfriend experience?"

'I'm afraid I don't know what that is.'

'Well, Zaveer can meet you in a bar or wherever, you can have a drink, like on a regular date, get to know each other.'

'No, I don't think I'll be needing that.'

'Sure. That'll be escort experience then.'

I gave her my credit card number and she assured me that when the bill appeared on the statement it would give no indication of being for an escort.

After the dinner, my publisher walked back to the hotel with me and we said goodnight in the lobby. Alone in my room, I was unsure how to greet Zaveer. What to wear? Then I remembered that the whole point of this was that I didn't have to look good or sexy so I settled for brushing my teeth. While I waited for Zaveer's knock I tried to remember the way H had spoken to the Russian woman years before in the bedroom he shared with Lucy.

I had agreed to the threesome to please H. I was indifferent to it, women aren't really my thing, but he loved the idea of combining his mistress with a tart. She looked much more like a professional than the women Sebastian used to take me to visit, tall and beautiful, heavily made-up, blow-dried hair. I don't remember what she said her name was. The 'threesome' part was a bit half-hearted — we patted at one another a bit and then H had sex with her on the bed. He had told her what to do very courteously, 'and now would you, please? . . . if you don't mind?' After he paid her, she went into the bathroom to dress. H sat behind me on the bed and brushed out my hair. The Russian woman saw him doing it as she left. It made me feel better than her.

Zaveer's hair was a bit darker than I'd fancied but otherwise he was as requested. Like B, he arrived with a little bag of kit, a rucksack from which he unpacked condoms, a lavender-scented candle and several bottles containing oil and lube. He asked me if I wanted him to start with a massage, to help me relax. I didn't, but in a polite tone similar to that in which H had spoken to the Russian prostitute I did ask him if he would mind doing kissing.

'That's optional, yes.'

It was the most relaxing and enjoyable sexual experience of my entire life. Not because we did anything I hadn't done a thousand times before, but because I felt under no pressure to please. I didn't have to encourage him or say porn words or do anything at all that I didn't want to do. I fucked him like a man, for as long as I felt like, which turned out to be not that long. When I was done there was still an hour on the clock.

'Now I want you to talk to me. Tell me how you got into this work.'

Zaveer said he was saving up to do his MA. He and a friend thought it would be a bit of a laugh to try escorting, but it hadn't worked out for the friend.

'How come?'

Before being allowed to work as escorts, the men had to do health checks, criminal records and so on, and then they were given a week-long training course. Some of it sounded like an old-fashioned finishing school, how to pull out a woman's chair or help her into a car, some of it was various sexual techniques and there was also a module on conversation and table manners. At the end of the week, candidates had to service a client in a room with a two-way mirror, watched by the owner of the agency, who was the lady I had spoken to on the phone earlier that day.

This was fascinating., 'Do the clients get a discount? Like when you get the trainee at the hairdressers?' I asked.

Zaveer didn't know, though he said it was a good question. He had been quite lucky, he explained, as the most difficult part of the job for a man was obviously getting aroused. His practice client had been an attractive woman who had enjoyed herself, but his mate had failed the test. His client had weighed over two hundred pounds and, try as he might, the friend couldn't get it up.

'The lady was mortified,' said Zaveer.

So there was no escape. Even if you were paying you could still be judged and found wanting.

Zaveer told me that the agency provided the condoms and massage oil, but that he had bought the lavender scented candle out of his own money because he thought it added a romantic touch. I would be receiving an email from the agency asking for customer satisfaction feedback, he said, though I could rest assured that it would ask about his services only in the most general terms. I said I would be sure to mention the lavender candle in the 'Additional Comments' section.

As Zaveer was leaving he gave me a card, 'in case you're ever in Melbourne again.'

'I know it's not your real name,' I said, 'but it's pronounced Xavier. Like in French.' That was a dickish thing to say, but then hadn't the whole point of the exercise been to behave like a dick?

Despite feeling very sorry for the mortified lady, I was exhilarated after Zaveer left. I thought I should tell all my friends; I could imagine myself becoming evangelical on the subject of male prostitutes. The moment of glee when the door closed and you could stretch out on the sheets alone. No snoring, no worrying about bad breath in the morning, no terrible dawn cab ride across the wastes of town with your knickers in your handbag. No cock tax! And think of the efficiency: no time wasted getting ready, no time trying to be charming and amusing, no emotional energy expended worrying if he liked you or liked you enough, no time thinking about him at all.

This felt like a wondrous and liberating revelation. No time thinking about him. At All. How economical too! Think of all the wasted money on waxing and manicures and underwear and shouting your half of dinner to show you are politically equal. So efficient! Quick, safe, clean: three hundred Australian dollars was a positive bargain. No wonder men had kept this for themselves so long. I had bought the flesh of another human being. I had subjugated them to my superior economic power. It felt delightful.

22. ABSENCE UNDER FIRE

Anne Clarke did not come to the house in Skagen that night. At 10 p.m. I locked the front door and went to bed with half a Zopi. Things were long past the point where I could even pretend to myself that I could sleep without pills. A walk in the morning. More waiting. I smoked until I retched, lighting more cigarettes through the metallic taint of my own guts. Last night in the lulling warmth of the stove I had yearned for Anne to come, a liquid longing which had fermented into sour anger. At 6 p.m. I was in my chair again; by 8 p.m. I was telling myself I'd have to wait another night. Then the doorbell rang.

I hadn't heard an engine or the sound of a car door. My book was in my lap. Anne Clarke was here and I had practically dozed off. I snapped off the lamp next to my chair. The bell rang again. I held my breath as the air around me shifted. She was opening the door. Two steps into the hallway. Then the kitchen door opened. I didn't move. Anne pulled the door to and I heard her make for the stairs. Her tread was heavy – she must be carrying a bag. I listened as she climbed the first flight, paused, then the steps grew fainter as she went up through the house. A thin stiletto of icy Danish air sliced through the fug of woodsmoke and tobacco in the kitchen from the open front door. I could smell her. A slight tang of cologne and beneath it something thicker, acrid. Whoever was in the house with me was not a woman.

It had to be the caretaker who had given me the keys in the port. He hadn't called out, but perhaps he had come to check the heating and thought I was out. The monumental stupidity of what I had contrived could wait. The front door was a few metres away,

I could still run. But the footsteps were descending. I switched on the lamp and feeling for the knife between the cushions, slid slowly, slowly, to my feet. The kitchen door opened. I was shaking so much I was going to drop the knife. I focused on the mirror in between the blue plates.

It was Mr Ali.

*

He came into the kitchen and walked right past me, down towards the door to the sitting room. He rattled the handle, but the chair was behind it. I moved for the doorway and kicked over the lamp.

He froze at the noise, turned around slowly, 'Ah. There you are.'

He didn't look mad or evil. He looked like Mr Ali, though without the red and black sweatshirt. He wore a thin tweed jacket, no gloves or scarf, a satchel across his chest. He was reaching into his pocket.

'Stay back. Stay there.' I croaked. I hadn't spoken aloud for two days, my voice was corrugated with cigarettes. I held up the knife so he could see its blade in the skewed light of the fallen lamp, 'Don't move.'

He reached out slowly and carefully placed some notes and coins at the far end of the kitchen island. 'I brought your change. There was a bus. I didn't want to waste money on a taxi.'

A feint. A taxi driver would have remembered him, the bus was more anonymous. Mr Ali looked very cold. I thought I could see little stalactites of ice in his thick moustache.

Still holding the knife in front of me, I reached round with my other hand for my phone. 'Don't move. Several people know I'm here. I'm going to leave and I'm going to call the police.' My voice was shaking. All of me was shaking.

'I'm sorry if I startled you. I didn't mean to. But you said you wouldn't call the police. If I came, that is. I'm here.'

'What?

'My wife, Salma. My wife has done a terrible thing.'

Mrs Ali was Salma. Salma was Anne Clarke?

'You'd better sit down.'

*

I made Mr Ali a cup of tea, and one for myself. I sat stooped with my head over the steam.

He held both hands round his mug, 'My wife thought that you and I . . . that we were having an affair.'

'Oh? Tell me more.'

'My wife is jealous. She is not British. When you moved into the house, she asked me about you.'

I had been in the shop every five minutes when I first moved into the neighbourhood, buying picture hooks and essential bits and pieces, and later the door chain and large brass hook for B's visits. I had made conversation with Mr Ali, found out about him being a theatre director. The day my books were delivered he had helped out with moving the heavy labelled boxes into position in front of the shelves. I had thought it was very kind of him.

'Salma didn't like it that you talked to me whenever you came into the shop. Then you gave me the theatre tickets, the ones from the newspaper. I was happy, I'd visited the Globe, but I'd never been to a play there. She refused to come with me. She said I shouldn't accept presents from strange women. I went anyway, and she was furious. Then she saw your picture on the front of a magazine in the newsagents. It was the Saturday supplement of *The Times*.'

The pictures involved bouffed hair, a short red Burberry trench, five-inch Louboutin boots and not much else. In the accompanying article, the journalist had described me as 'petite and doll-like'.

'Salma looked you up, online. She saw all the pictures of you, the things you had written.'

I knew what she would have seen. *Bitch. Slut. Whore.*

'She told me she started spying on you, walking up and down outside the Swedish Church. She said different men came to your flat and you drew the curtains in the afternoons. She knew I had never been there, apart from that day with the books, but she said it showed what sort of woman you are. Dangerous. Bad. Then, for a long time, she stopped mentioning you and I thought she had got over her suspicions. But you rang me, before Christmas, quite late at night, about your key.'

I thought back to Daniel doing his Milk Tray Man act through my window.

'I save all the customers' numbers if they use the key service, so I know it's them calling. I was asleep, but she saw the light on the screen of my phone, with your name. Salma crept out of the house and went round to your flat. She saw you and your daughter going inside, so she thought you couldn't be calling about a key. She said she wanted to speak to you but your daughter was with you. So then she started watching you again. She wrote down what you did, what time you left the house, she learned your routines.'

Go, Salma.

'Two days ago, when she was sure you would be out, she took your master key from the locker. She knows the combination. I'd sometimes asked her to fetch keys for customers if I was away. She went to your flat and . . .'

'I know what she did.'

'It was the books. She thought that would upset you. She knew how I had felt when I lost all my books. And she says she wrote a message.'

I showed him the note on the kitchen worktop: *PLEASE STAY AWAY FROM MY HUSBAND.*

'Yes. Salma wrote that. I told her about you barging into the shop, how upset you were. She said at first she felt glad, but then she began to worry. She was ashamed. So the next day she went to try to speak to you. There was a taxi waiting outside and she saw you putting the envelope under the plant.'

The woman in the headscarf.

'She waited until you left, then took the envelope and came to me. That's when she explained everything. So I had to come. Salma is terrified you will report her to the police.'

'Why didn't she come herself?'

'She cannot leave England. She has no passport. If she were to get into trouble with the police she'd be deported. We thought that's what you were doing, making her come to this place to catch her. A Catch 22?'

'That would have been . . . ingenious.'

'Please. Salma is very sorry and knows she has made a terrible mistake. But please, please don't go to the police.'

'So Salma thought you and I were fucking?' I used the word deliberately, I wanted to offend him. 'And she broke into my house. But how does she explain these?' I picked up the notebook and showed him the transcriptions of Anne Clarke's emails.

'Salma has been writing to me. It's been going on for years. Threatening me, harassing me. How does she explain that?'

'What is this?'

'I wrote down . . . never mind. Look.'

I opened my phone and typed 'Anne Clarke' into the search box above my email, 'Look. These are her emails.'

'Salma could not have written these. She hardly speaks English.'

'I thought you said she looked me up online? Read things I had written?'

'She asked our daughter to translate them. She is only thirteen.'

'Call Salma now and ask her for details. I want to know the truth.'

'My phone plan doesn't have international calls. I'm sorry.'

'Oh, Christ. OK. Use mine. What's Salma's number?' I punched it in and handed him the phone. I heard her voice and there was a rapid conversation in Arabic.

'Ask her about the note.'

'She used a dictionary.'

Please. Please stay away from my husband. It had seemed off, style-wise. Implausibly humble for Anne Clarke. I groaned. Anne Clarke had responded to my request to meet her in Hyde Park. She had stood me up. Had she attempted to follow my next instructions, come to the house? But she wouldn't have found the envelope under the aluminium pot because Salma had taken it. Anne Clarke was still out there.

'Give me my phone! No one's getting deported. Tell Salma . . . Just give me the phone!'

'Where are you?' I typed to Anne Clarke's email address.
After thirty seconds, my inbox pinged. 'Undelivered Mail: It has not been possible to deliver your email . . .'

Anne Clarke was gone.

*

Mr Ali helped me to put back the mop and chair and mirror and plates. He set the table while I cooked. We ate the smoked eel with pickled cucumber and green peppercorns, rare steak with dill sauce and small boiled potatoes then the *crème brulée*, with two bottles of the Danish man's Gaia. I told him about Anne Clarke and the black notebook and Giovanni Piccolo, about all I had discovered and believed and feared. He thought that my last email, where I threatened to report her to the police, must have scared her off.

'But why all this?' he gestured at the kitchen, 'Why come all the way here? Did you believe that she would do what you asked?'

My plan had seemed smart at the time. Extreme but not dumb.

'Whoever she was, she wanted to *know*. I thought if she was prepared to do this, as I was, we could finally have an honest encounter. Or something.'

After dinner we sat by the wood burner with the last of the wine. Mr Ali asked me politely about my writing but I didn't have a whole lot to say about that, so I told him a lexical joke that amused me: 'Taper' is French for 'to type', as on a keyboard, but 'se taper', the reflexive, can mean various things: to be stuck with something, to consume something or, colloquially, to have sex, of which the best translation would be 'to have it off'. The sense makes its way into English with 'to tup', to turn upside down. A 'tup' can be a male sheep, a ram, and 'to tup' can also mean to have sex. So writing and fucking flip the world topsy-turvy.

'Like in *Othello*,', said Mr Ali, 'An old black ram is tupping your white ewe.'

Mr Ali talked about Shakespeare's comedies. Told me that in his opinion *A Midsummer Night's Dream* was a cruel play because it reveals how mercurial love is. There is no sound base to it, only a trick of the sight, an illusion effected by a few drops of flower juice on the eyelids. We believe that we love, but that feeling can vanish as quickly as it appears, without explanation and we are left wandering like Hermia in the woods, bereft and bewildered. I picked up my copy of Nancy Mitford's *The Pursuit of Love* and read him some of the last part where Fanny is speaking to her mother, known as the Bolter for her serial love affairs. She talks about the death of her friend Linda, who has skipped gaily through the story from one husband to another before dying in childbirth:

'But Fanny,' said the Bolter, 'don't you think perhaps it's just as well? The lives of women like Linda and me are not so much fun when one begins to grow older.'

'But I think she would have been happy with Fabrice,' said Fanny. 'He was the great love of her life, you know.'

'Oh dulling,' replied the Bolter sadly, 'One always thinks that. Every, every time.'

Mr Ali and I watched the last log in the stove burn down to white embers, then we went upstairs to our rooms at the top of the house and slept the sleep of the just.

23. THE NOTEBOOK REVISITED

I didn't see Mr Ali after we took the flight back from Denmark together. Nor did I ever get to meet Salma. We hadn't shared dinner or velvety Gaia or warm conversation. Mr Ali hadn't been interested when I tried to explain about Anne Clarke, he had said exhaustedly that it was none of his business and went to bed, leaving me to stare at the stove alone. When he described what Salma had done, he seemed almost proud, as though her jealousy and impulsiveness were something to be expected from a decent woman, a proper wife. I felt sullied by his contempt. I had behaved hysterically.

Soon after I returned from Skagen, my daughter and I moved away from London. I couldn't afford it any longer; besides, I was done with it and it was done with me. Before we left, I took the diamond bracelet H had given me to a jeweller's in Leather Lane and sold it. While the owner was cheating me, I noticed a box of tissues on the table, the divorce-lawyer-therapist kind. I walked a couple of doors down to the William Hill betting shop and put the money on a horse. I picked the racetrack at random and selected the runner from the jockey's colours: black, red and yellow. It didn't come in.

Sorting through the papers in my trunk in preparation for the move I came across an issue of the *Times Literary Supplement* folded in clear plastic. It was a complimentary copy, sent to contributors when they have had a review published. On page six was the article I had written about the book which had been launched at the party in Mayfair where the Blonde Terrapin made her remarks about me. The number had been published the previous autumn, when Anne

Clarke had emailed me to ask why I didn't stick to writing my 'own sleazy books'.

Anne Clarke had been referring to the review. Giovanni Piccolo and the plagiarism case had nothing to do with her. However, I had convinced myself to the contrary. It had not been Emma or Polly or Lucy who had schemed to bring me low. There had been no elaborate alibi, no concerted, slow-worked plan.

The card from F which he signed 'your secret friend' joined *Tricks for Thrifters!* in the dustbin when we left. The black notebook I kept.

*

In our new house, I have a writing desk for the first time. The house is very old and very shabby, but the desk is a beautiful piece. It is dark cherry wood, curved like a sickle moon, with a panel in the centre, lined in cracked green leather, and a cupboard on either side. Another curved section backs the top, divided into twelve cubby holes. The desk is placed next to the door to the garden, above which grows a jasmine garland which runs the length of the house and so far has survived my ungreen fingers. In the garden there is a Byzantine well of white stone and a pomegranate tree.

The black notebook is in the right-hand cupboard, which has its own key, attached to a dark red tassel. For a long time, I could not look at it. Then one evening in spring when the jasmine was just coming into flower I unlocked the cupboard and carried the notebook into the garden. My daughter was staying over with one of her new friends. She had left Emmeline with me for company. I poured a glass of wine and began to read.

Twilight falls swiftly in this sea-bound city. In my garden with its high walls the light vanishes in a snap. I had only read a few pages from the notebook in which I had written about my lovers' wives when I had to get up and fetch candles. Bent over the book, slapping at mosquitoes, I read on until I came to the passages about Belle de Jour.

Anne Clarke's story was written in the order in which it happened. Around it I had recorded my memories of H, F and B and their wives, of Sebastian, of the things which had happened to me which detached me so far from myself. I had been so engaged with discovering Anne Clarke that I had been blind to something else, something wrong. I had to go back indoors, boot up my laptop on the cherrywood desk, wait for the Wi-Fi signal to creep through the five-hundred-year-old walls. I needed to consult the magazine, *The Bookseller*, which reports all the behind-the-scenes news of the publishing business: which books have been acquired by which firms, which authors have changed representation, auctions, rights deals. There were some dates I had to confirm. When I found them I closed my computer and went back to the garden. I blew out the candles and sat there in the dark.

*

When Sebastian died, his agent was the man who had introduced me to F in the Soho gutter. Before that though, when he had first signed the contract for his book, his literary agent had been Horace Chisholm. The man who had represented Belle de Jour.

'You're the girl from Whitstable.'

I had thought Sebastian had remembered me, that our meeting had been as delicious and inevitable as a first kiss. All the details in the *Sunday Times* article, which I was convinced my friend Ellie had supplied, had come from him, the things I had confided, week after week as we ate cakes and read poems. That was where the black notebook had brought me, in the end. My beloved friend had betrayed me.

What had I expected? Honour amongst thieves? Had Sebastian been in on it to try to ingratiate himself with Horace Chisholm? Or just because he thought it was funny to set up his dazzled little acolyte in the press? Obviously, I am the sort of woman who does writers. I had set out deliberately to attract those married men, making myself into a caricature as I had done in all those sex articles I had written, in the photographs for which I had posed with Sebastian. I had made myself into a story to amuse him, but then had I not lived much of my life in the third person?

Anne Clarke had written to me across a divide. She wanted me to know that she existed, that she mattered. Her feelings were real whereas I was too 'cold' to have any. I had envied her righteous conviction just as I had envied Sebastian's uncompromising life. If Anne Clarke was Emma or Polly or Lucy, then she had ultimately denied those feelings. She had played with me, poked at me, but she hadn't actually done anything about the fact that I had fucked her husband. B and H and F were all still married. My own fear and guilt and shame had done the rest. It occurred to me that I despised Anne Clarke for her dishonesty as much as she did me for mine.

Sebastian hadn't believed in my feelings either. It wasn't

anything to get angry about; he didn't have any of his own, as he was the first to admit. I had loved Sebastian to the end. Perhaps it was a little, timorous love, but I had believed in it. That felt quite a small thought. I tried a bigger one. 'I would not have done that . . . I would not have done that.'

*

In the days when I was still running, when I was winning a race, there was a feeling in the last few seconds where I felt that my spikes no longer touched the ground. I was weightless, way out in front, nothing but the air in my face and the tape before me. I wasn't always set wrong.

*

In the cubbyholes of the desk there are, from right to left:
- A postcard from the National Gallery of Velasquez's *Rokeby Venus* with a message from my mother on the back.
- A leather notebook for quotations.
- My cigarette case and lighter.
- A matchbook from Tangier with a picture of blue and white tiles.
- Skip one.
- An origami boat painted gold inside made by my daughter.
- A wooden model of a sleeping mouse, another gift from my daughter.
- A silver snuff box.

- A seed pod from the Oman desert.
- A papier mâché box with a pressed oak leaf on the lid, containing my great-grandmother's wedding ring.
- An orange plastic alarm clock.

The skipped cubbyhole holds a piece of writing paper with flowers printed round the edges. On it I have written Graham Greene's three criteria for being a writer: 'Disloyalty', 'Freedom from Accepted Opinions' and 'A Taste for Treason'.

Anne Clarke was real. I have her words in those six emails. I have the postcard from the National Gallery which she delivered to my house in London. I never did discover whether she was one of my lovers' wives.

Perhaps, now, I will.

Printed in Great Britain
by Amazon